Breakfast with Kamuzu

11/6/2011

Dear Barrett —

Thanks for visiting Albuquerque! This may bring back memories.

All My Best!

9+ a all

Breakfast with Kamuzu
By Hubert A. Allen, Jr.

Published by:
Hubert Allen and Associates
720-25 Tramway Lane NE, Albuquerque
   NM 87122   U.S.A.

Copyright © 2000 by Hubert A. Allen, Jr.
720-25 Tramway Lane NE, Albuquerque
      New Mexico   87122   USA
Tel:(505)797-3520; Fax:(505)797-3521;
E-mail: hubertaallen@compuserve.com

First Edition 2001
Prepared in the United States of America

Publisher's Cataloging-in-Publication

Allen, Hubert A.
   Breakfast with Kamuzu / Hubert A. Allen, Jr. -- 1st ed.
   p. cm.
   Includes bibliographic references.
   ISBN 0-9641694-4-4

   1. Malawi--History--Fiction. 2. Afro-Americans--History--Fiction.   I. Title.

PS3501.L535B74 2001   813'.54
                        QBI00-900575

TABLE OF CONTENTS

Map of Africa 1890
About the Time of Kamuzu Banda's Birth

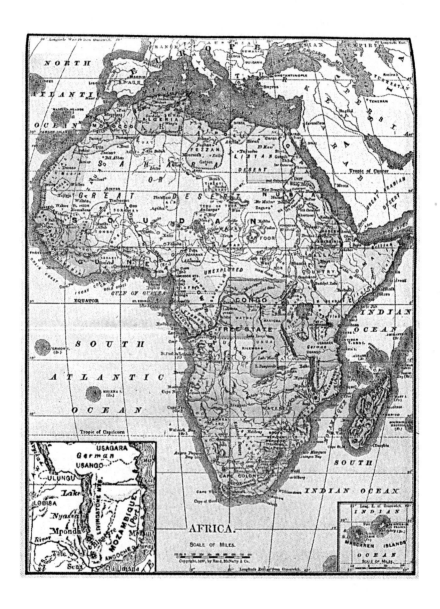

His Excellency's Departure

The stadium bulged with ten thousand ebony skinned Africans. At the foot of the stands the Party regulars, big African men wearing identical black suits with dark brown pinstripes, controlled the action. Thousands of well-behaved school children wearing uniforms of white shirts and navy blue skirts or trousers were seated.

The most colorfully dressed were the women, in wrap-around skirts bearing *his* face; not that of an octogenarian but as it looked some thirty years ago. The packed stadium waited in anticipation for the appearance of their self-styled President for Life, Dr. Hastings Kamuzu Banda, *Ngwazi* or Savior of the Malawian people.

I was the only white face in the crowd, an outsider, an American. I heard that foreigners were welcome to attend Kamuzu's send-off for annual crop inspection and I accepted the offer, apparently the only one. In the Central Region events began at the stadium adjacent to his palace in Lilongwe, the capital city of the African nation of Malawi.

The chatter from the people was loud and musical, and although I was the only stranger, I did not fear at all for my safety, as Kamuzu told his people to respect the visitors. He only tolerated such outsiders because we were invited, a small group of experts, here to supplement the small Malawian technocracy. Over ninety percent of the people lived rural, agricultural, subsistence lives. Crops were of paramount importance.

The annual crop inspection took place in January, which south of the equator is summer, beginning at the south end of the long, thin country and moving northwards over a period of several weeks. Lilongwe was in the Central Region. It was a hot day, though it was still early, and a bright, cloudless sky spread over the stadium like a great flowing sea. It was not known exactly when His Excellency would appear, but today he was heading far into the countryside, and time would be of the essence.

5

All the beautiful children, all their parents and most of their grandparents had grown up knowing only this one leader, Dr. Hastings Kamuzu Banda. He brought them freedom from the British colonialists who had jailed him for a year. But by 1960, the freedom movement was alive in many colonies and independence was spreading across Africa like a bush fire and he was released.

It was a phased national freedom. It might have gone slower except that the British made the tactical mistake of combining Malawi, then Nyasaland, with Southern and Northern Rhodesia into one larger Central African Federation in the 1950s. The indignity of being lumped together with the more prosperous neighbors was even more odious than being colonial subjects of the Queen. Such a loss of identity was intolerable and Dr. Hastings Kamuzu Banda was summoned back to Nyasaland by his people. He was the only one who could lead them to freedom.

Africa is sweet with smells and the stadium was no exception. In the air floated an invisible smoke, a combination of burning wood and rotting organic matter which made a kind of aphrodisiac. The people, for their part, had made efforts to be washed and clean for the occasion. Many smelled of soap. Here soap was not just used as a cleanser to be rinsed off the body, it was laid on like talcum powder. But the heat was coming on strong and I, unused to the heat, was sweating like a monsoon rain. Doubtlessly, I smelled bad to the Africans.

Suspense was building. I felt it in the air. Then another sound; dull at first, increasing to a persistent buzzing and then a loud rumble, until a mechanical roar filled the air. I looked everywhere for the source. Suddenly, over the top of the stadium wall came a giant, black helicopter, a beast stranger than any produced in Africa. It moved to the center of the stadium. Hovering for a moment, it then came down wobbly, to the middle, kicking up dust in a murky brown swirl. The front end dipped, the back tail balanced out, and its three wheels touched ground. The high pitch sound softened when the motor was cut, and dust began to settle as the great insect landed and the three previously invisible rotors appeared.

It was a moment of tremendous incongruity. A twentieth century contraption landing in a nineteenth century agrarian world. The highest form of technology in a place nearly devoid of machines. When the motor finally ceased and the dust settled, there remained a quizzical feeling. Did the black machine have a life of its own? Was there someone or something inside? For a moment the answer was unclear and the helicopter sat lifelessly.

Then a door swung open and a short ladder slid down to the ground. A form in a black leather uniform and a gleaming helmet stepped down awkwardly. The spectral creature took center stage as all eyes looked fast upon it. The beast reached the ground, took two steps forward and stopped. Two limbs reached up, took hold and twisted the black orb on top until it lifted off, revealing a ghostly white human face. Someone whispered that he was a French pilot.

The mood returned to celebration and the Malawians went back to their happy chatter. Now I was really sweating buckets, getting hungry and thirsty. There were no concession stands in the stadium, although street vendors set up stands where they sold peanuts (called ground nuts), cigarettes, mangos, papaya, and warm sodas. But, once inside the stadium you had to stay, and I had nothing with me to eat or drink.

I was getting restless when a silence swept over the crowd, and a large gateway opened at one end of the stadium. A few of the Party men stepped out into the field, waved to and organized a flock of women gathered near-by. Then a black limousine crept into the stadium and stopped about five car lengths from the helicopter.

A moment passed when everyone stood still and quiet. A hulking Malawi Congress Party man walked over to the back door of the limo, pulled it open, and stepped back behind it deferentially. In seeming contrast to all the bigness of Africa; the huge stadium, the gigantic helicopter, the vast open sky above, a

7

diminutive figure in a dark black suit with an exceptionally tall top hat stepped out of the limo. It was Dr. Hastings Kamuzu Banda, President for Life of Malawi.

The crowd exploded in cheers and clapping hands. Women ululated at the top of their lungs, sending a musical wail bouncing back and forth across the stadium like echoes off a mountain. The children rooted, and the Party men urged them all on, pulling cheers out of the air with open hands and drawn fingers.

I was astounded. This small, frail, elderly man was known throughout Africa as the Big Man of Malawi, the one who ruled his people with an iron fist.

He raised up his famous lion-tail fly whisk; ivory handle and fluffy-topped switch, and thrashed violently at the air in a back and forth motion. The crowd loved it and cheered even louder. He slowly turned a full circle addressing all the people in the stadium with his ceremonial fly whisk.

After a moment that seemed to last an hour, Kamuzu turned his attention to a group of women specially gathered in the field who were prepared to dance for His Excellency. Like all women in Malawi, they were said to be part of Kamuzu's *mbumba* - he was the chiefly father of them all. These women were dressed in the colorful wrap-around skirts, *chitenje* as they are called, which had imprinted on them the face of their ruler and the many accomplishments attributed to him since independence. Among the highlights featured on the colorful cotton cloth was the Kamuzu International Airport, the capital city of Lilongwe, the University of Malawi, and the Kachere-Chiweta road. The roots of agrarian Malawi were also shown: maize (*chimanga*), tobacco (*fodya*), and cotton (*thonje*), all focal to today's events.

It was not until 1964 that Malawi became truly an independent nation. Where violence stood out in the freedom struggles of many other African countries, this was not the case in Malawi, where Kamuzu Banda peacefully negotiated the freedom of his people. There were some tragic deaths among the Africans and a minor riot or two in Blantyre, but no war between the colonized and the colonizer. The *chitenje* boldly claimed "30 Glorious Years with Kamuzu," harking back to his return in 1958. The women began to chant and dance as *Kamuzu* focused on them. Slowly, he stepped backwards towards the waiting helicopter, fanning his fly whisk with vigor, the women's dancing equaling his pace. Step after slow step backwards, seconds upon historic seconds, the country and its leader danced as one, a cotillion of freedom, respect and submission.

In a few ecstatic moments, Dr. Hastings Kamuzu Banda reached the short ramp leading into the helicopter. He stopped for one last glance at the throng of people, waved the fly whisk with assurance and then disappeared into the great black machine. The crowd roared with satisfaction. The door slammed shut. Silver blades began to rotate. Dust and leaves swirled with blinding fury, as the Big Man of Malawi took off into the heavens.

Breakfast with Kamuzu

The Bottom Hospital

Towards the end of the 1980s, consequence of the U.S. Government's concerned about the Cold War struggle in Africa, the Malawi Ministry of Health received a dozen computers and one trainer - me. I had pined for this job, a dream come true, a chance to live and work in Africa.

Malawi is a small country, located in the southeastern part of Africa, at the south end of the Great Rift Valley. Lake Malawi is a prominent body of fresh water which fills this end of the Great Rift Valley. Most of the land of Malawi is to the west of the lake, although the most populous areas in the Southern Region of the country are in the Shire River Valley.

The modern capital, Lilongwe, was carved out of the jungle and a few small villages. It has a modern, inverted pyramid shaped building, a stately campus of government ministries, a fine road system and modern housing.

The "Health Information Section," where I worked was located down at the Bottom Hospital, the old colonial hospital, now upstaged by the modern Kamuzu Hospital but still in use. I set up a training room in a long, one-story building with cracked cement walls and termite eaten doors in a section reserved for administrators. The room was not ideal for the computers; the humidity was too high, the dust omnipresent. Ants crept into the disk drives and sauntered across the keyboards, but this was the allotted space and we made the best of it by constantly sweeping and damp-mopping it down.

Outside the hospital building, families of the patients made camp. As is true in most African countries, food is not provided by the hospital and it is the duty, indeed necessity, of relatives to feed, wash and otherwise care for their sick. The hospital provides medicine, surgery, nursing. Many diseases thrive here that are absent in America: crippling polio, lock-jaw from tetanus, bulging goiter due to lack of iodine, schistosomes turning urine bloody red.

11

Like an obstacle course through Purgatory, I walked this gauntlet each day when I came to work.

Danny, my African assistant, was a wire- thin man of twenty, who spoke four African languages and had earned a university degree. I quickly discovered that he was an intense learner, driven to master the technology and willing to put endless hours to the task, despite monthly wages that wouldn't get an American to work for a day. He was my counter-part and the first person with whom I shared my knowledge and expertise.

For several months he and I worked together to put a computer curriculum together for the ministry. There were several key areas we chose to cover. Highest among our priorities was the use of simple spreadsheet technology; the mechanical adding and subtracting of figures for budgets. Word processing was essential for memos, manuals, written policies. Statistical packages were to help summarize the use of hospital and clinic services.

The second important Malawian was my administrator, Hexy Temba, who came highly recommended for his accounting acumen. Hexy was a round-shaped man, constantly sweating, with low-set, beady eyes and a quick tongue. He ruled the financial books.

The secretary was a young woman named Jane who quickly learned word processing and was a good organizer. Jane was connected, her father was an ambassador and it never hurt to have some people around with a little clout.

That was my team. Together we aspired to create a corps of computer literate Malawians who could bring the poor agrarian country into the Information Age, skipping the Industrial Age by necessity and circumstance.

Echoes Past

I lived in a house at the foot of Nkohma Mountain with five bedrooms and a staff of six. My home was luxurious by American and Malawian standards. A choice of three bathtubs in which I could stretch out my full six-foot frame, bright glowing electric lights which no neighboring village had, and the extra freezer for imported meats. I often felt embarrassed at the opulence.

With the house came a cook named Nelson, a housegirl named Beauty, uniformed guards twenty-four hours a day, a gardener and a driver named Viswell. The two acres of land were fenced, gaited, and manicured to a tee.

Such luxury had its price. Lack of privacy for one. There simply was not an instant when I was alone until the last moments of night. There was always a person around, accidentally opening a door I was hiding behind for a moment's reprieve, or an emergency which only I could resolve.

With a staff of six came the constant need for personnel management. My many roles included paymaster, lending institution, medicine man, surrogate uncle, and, worst of all, a "master" to my staff. The Malawians were polite, almost too polite and it took some time to get used to this deference. Perhaps the hardest thing to adjust to was being called "master." For days and days after first establishing the house I had asked Nelson, the cook, not to call me "master."

"Nelson, please don't call me master."

"Yes, master."

"Nelson, please, please don't call me master."

"Yes master."

It got to the point where I positively shook with frustration.

"Nelson, don't call me master!"

"Yes master."

"Why on earth are you calling me master? I can't stand that term." To an American, under the circumstances of our

13

contrasting economic circumstances and races, it reminded me of the Old South where masters owner slaves.

"I am very sorry, master."

Finally, at the height of exasperation, Nelson came to my rescue after I explained why the term was so offensive to me.

"When we say 'master,' master," he explained, "we mean master of the house, not master of slaves."

"Fine, okay but can we use another term?"

"To me, I like the term bwana, it means boss."

"That would be preferable, please share this change with all the staff."

"Yes master."

Well, I supposed, it was going to take some time for all of us to adjust to cultural differences, but most of the effort would have to come from me. I wanted to contribute to this land so far from home, yet I was not sure of the best path.

Banda's Youth

The legendary rise to power of Hastings Kamuzu Banda begins when he was a small boy in Kasungu District, in the Central Region of the British Protectorate of Nyasaland, as Malawi was known in colonial times. The year of his birth is uncertain, his age was never officially released, but it is thought to have occurred sometime around the start of the Twentieth Century, perhaps even a few years before. The Chewa name "Kamuzu" means "Little Root" after the shaman's medicine which cured his mother of infertility and led to his birth.

At the time, Kasungu District contained the barest thread of Western Civilization in the otherwise vast spool of Africa's interior. In fact, the contact between Africa and Europe was scarcely a quarter century old. That thread was crafted by the world renowned explorer, the Scottish missionary David Livingstone.

Kamuzu Banda was born to a typical African family and coincidentally near to one of the few Scottish mission stations in all of Africa. The influence was dramatic. Young Kamuzu was educated by the missionaries to read and write as the Europeans did. His first name, Hastings, was taken by Kamuzu Banda in his youth out of respect for the missionaries who educated him.

He was raised and initiated into the Chewa tradition at the age of about thirteen. This initiation was kept secret from the missionaries who frowned at such indigenous rituals. At dawn on his initiation day, his head was shaved and he was fed a large meal meant to last him a day or more. Then he left the hut of his family forever and was led into the bush. Blindfolded, and stripped naked, he had to promise never to reveal details of the coming ceremony or face a penalty of death.

When the blindfold was lifted, he saw whirling around him strange dancers with black, wooden masks, splattered with red paint, and wearing bark cloth robes. He was told by the organizer of the ceremony, a man with a fierce, intimidating countenance on his face, that these were the spirits of his ancestors.

Soon the initiation trial began. The young boy's hands and feet were tied and Kamuzu was strung upside down from a tree. A fire was lit underneath and then the spirit beings swung the bound, terrified initiate back and forth over the fire while reciting a litany of minor offenses he had committed in village life.

Eventually, he passed out. When he awoke he was alone in one of the secluded huts in which initiates must live for two months. During this time a traditional teacher came to instruct Kamuzu Banda, now a Chewa man, with the code, ethics, and morality of the Chewa way.

The effect of these dual influences, traditional African and Scottish missionary, produced in young Kamuzu Banda, a character combining the strengths of both worlds with unusual ambition.

Nyasaland was never a major destination for colonists. In the southern part of the country, where white-run estate farming occurred, there was an odious practice along the lines of apartheid, called *thangata*. In the North where Kamuzu was raised, because of David Livingstone, religion had a greater influence on the relationship between Europeans and Nyasas.

Legend tells us that, at the age of about fourteen, Hastings Banda set off alone and on foot for the Republic of South Africa to better himself. A thousand mile walk; pestered by lions, tortured by insects, penniless but keenly ambitious, he survived the trek.

Africa's Longest Rock Climb

My hidden agenda for Malawi was to climb its mountains like no person had ever climbed them before. There was a climbing history. The British began rock climbing here in the late 1950's and a few rock climbing routes were established. There was even a guidebook with published route descriptions for the most interesting spot in the country, the Mulanje Massif in the Southern Region. The guidebook claimed that the West Face of Chambe Peak, one of the peaks at the edge of the massif, was the longest rock climb in Africa - 5,500 vertical feet. At the time of my arrival, it had never been successfully climbed.

It was a figure I had to read twice, "5,500 vertical feet." To comprehend this claim, I reached for a familiar comparison. Yosemite Valley, California, a place where I had climbed several times, had the longest rock face in the Continental United States - El Capitan at 3,300 vertical feet. Yosemite also had Half Dome at 2,000 vertical feet. Yes, that was the comparison, Half Dome on top of El Capitan, add a couple of hundred feet at the top and drop it in the middle of Africa. Gasp! I had to see it for myself.

The journey by car to Mulanje took one full day, mostly along the M1 highway, the country's central artery. Two lanes cut through a wild, sparsely populated countryside. Like most Saturdays, the sides of the road were lined with villagers making their way to market centers to sell articles such as clay pots, charcoal, and foods that were produced in the villages. I shared the road with a rare bicyclist, and sometimes a manned wagon pulled by oxen. Occasionally I stopped the car while herdsmen, usually a couple of young boys, cajoled their cattle across the road. It was dangerous driving at best, worsened by the roadside traffic. One aberrant cow, hit at 100 klicks an hour, would spell a nasty end to the adventure.

Driving down a thin, paved tarmac ribbon, I moved through gorgeous scenery of rocky precipices, rounded valleys, and broad plains. One hour south, I reached Dedza where pine forests covered jutting mountains. To the western side of the road was the Mozambique border. A burnt out building with faint Portuguese writing on its facade told the story of a painful civil war; raging, destroying, spreading suffering for more than a decade now. As I looked west there were no people, no villages, and no hope in sight.

At Liwonde I stopped to view the Shire River which emptied from Lake Chilwa. It was too late, or too early in the day, to see hippos or crocodiles but I knew they lurked under murky waters.

From the river valley, the road climbed into highlands. Mushroom men were out, selling the huge fungi, big as plates, for eating. I drove through another forest and soon into the town of Zomba, a tree-lined shady oasis, with a view of the Zomba Plateau and its several rocky buttresses above.

I stopped at a bakery and bought fresh buns with flour sprinkled on top and an ice cold coke. I was getting weary, but there were miles more before I would see the Mulanje Massif and the West Face of Chambe Peak. I steeled myself to press on, for I had to see that face today.

After a section of busy, dangerous road, I approached Blantyre, the commercial capital. I came to a stately brick clocktower and then I cut to the east towards Limbe, famous for tobacco auctions. I began to feel a tug, pulling me to an unknown but powerful destiny. The West Face of Chambe, longest rock climb in Africa, had been a grave to at least one party.

The story of the ill-fated party was sketchy. Two British climbers attempted the West Face five years previous. They came to Malawi with fanfare and half a ton of equipment. The Africans said it couldn't be climbed. At Likabula Forestry Station, they were given a last warning - no one had ever climbed that face. They hired a reluctant team of porters to get them to a base camp.

There they eyed a route and began up the wall one late July morning. That is the best time to climb Mulanje, cool but not cold, without rain. The team explained to the porters that they planned to top out in five to six days and that the porters were to break camp and walk up the backside to meet the climbers.

Five days passed. For three nights villagers on the Phalombe Plains saw lights on the face of Chambe. For five days the porters waited on top. Then a sixth day, a seventh, and after a faithful fortnight, they gave up. The climbers were never seen again.

I reached the village of Mulanje, a short strip of tin buildings. Nearby I saw the massive flank of Mulanje Massif - Manga Peak and other steep escarpments whose names I did not know. The massif's daunting walls continued northward and I cut onto the Mulanje-Phalombe dirt road and drove parallel to the massif where the West Face of Chambe could be seen.

Bumping down the dirt road, I accelerated, even though I should have slowed down. The car bounced and scraped along the dirt, lifting a veil of red dust into the air behind me. The roller coaster road bordered luxuriant green, manicured tea estates. Fields extended high up towards the base of the massif and I saw the African workers plucking tea leaves and depositing them into the large white sack each of them wore on their backs, held into place by a band around their foreheads

After about ten kilometers, I began to see the profile of Chambe Peak itself - rearing harshly skyward in a two-step mass of solidity. Soon the car came squarely in front of the wall. I stopped along the side of the road after a skid, sending a cloud of red dust skyward. I stepped out of the car and gawked at the West Face of Chambe Peak looming before me - a ridiculously large mountain of rock. This was beyond any cliff size I had known before. The humongous face made my heart beat strongly, and my flesh burn with ambition to be the first to climb the greatest rock face in Africa. Climbing ambition is a rare and beautiful human folly, one must take advantage of these moments.

Craning my neck, I visually followed a thin black line in the lower wall. As a climber I knew that in reality this was probably a chimney, something like a three-sided elevator shaft about as wide as a man's body (my binoculars revealed this to be true). It cut up the bottom two-thousand feet of the wall like a black dagger. The lower wall eased back to a huge ledge and then the 3,500 feet of upper wall thrust skyward like the steepest skyscraper - but it was much, much taller than anything ever built by humanity. This was the West Face of Chambe Peak - my holy grail of climbing.

Looking upwards and imagining a human passage up the wall, I took a silent pledge to climb the face. With whom? I had no partner. When? I had a year to go in Malawi. Could I climb the longest rock face in Africa and survive? Seeing the great unclimbed rock, rising more than a vertical mile, I felt the profound smallness of a frail, transient human being in the presence of nature's mightiest. Humility was in order today, but to cast my bid and climb a rock wall of this magnitude I needed something else - audacity.

An Interest

Meanwhile training at the Ministry of Health was going better than I expected. Danny proved not only a learned counterpart but also tireless at the task. This left me time for other activities. One of my favorites was popping over to the United Nations Development Program for tea with a particularly fetching intern from New York who was responsible for their housing program.

Karen was a striking woman; tall and thin with glossy jet black hair and very red lipstick. She was unattached like many of the expatriates in Malawi and found the outward politeness of the Malawians unmatched by social interactions. This was partly because there was an incipient paranoia about foreigners, despite the need to have some of us in country. Many drivers were said to be spies, willing to pass on the most casual off-color remark about government to the authorities. I learned there were standing orders for civil servants not to socialize with expatriates. A cozy dinner with a colleague could mean the loss of a job.

Of course, there were the back alleys for entertainment, the bars and bar girls, but that was risky business. The AIDS epidemic was quietly spreading throughout Africa and Malawi was along one of the main conduits, the Cape to Cairo route. Government did not acknowledge the problem at the time but, being at the Ministry of Health, rumors were rampant. The thinning disease, the curse, the local name was *edzi*, and it was becoming all too well known along the M1 roadway where the disease passed from transcontinental trucker to bar girl to local villager and back again and down the road. In short, intimate relationships with locals were out.

The United Nations offices were spanking new. Karen had lived in-country longer than I and had real insight into the people and the land. She was hopelessly in love with Africa, but I aimed to sway her my way. When we met for tea, she always wore a fresh flower in her hair. It became a little joke between us.

"Is that gardenia today?"

"Very good, you seem to be getting more sensitive."

"I'm learning about beautiful scents from our all too infrequent visits together," I said, taking her hand in greeting, a small, smooth, manicured hand with red polished nails.

We sat in her comfortable office, curtains drawn to keep out the fierce afternoon sun. A secretary brought in a tray with two cups, a pot of tea, milk, sugar and a few biscuits. I watched Karen's slender hand gracefully pour the tea. It seemed her every motion was graceful.

"How's the training going?" she asked.

"We've got courses going regularly now. Danny is great. He does all the teaching." I sipped at the tea and looked up at her blue eyes and long black lashes.

"What's your favorite place in Malawi?" I asked her. She seemed to know everything about the place, and in her job she traveled a lot.

"Kasungu National Park, I love the game viewing."

"Isn't that the district were H.E. is from?" I asked, using the expatriate vernacular for His Excellency.

"Yes, he has a palace there, but he doesn't go very often any more."

"Why?"

"Rumor is that he thinks it's haunted."

"Haunted?" I asked incredulously.

"That's what they say." She sipped her tea, picked up a small plate and offered me a biscuit (or cookie as we Americans usually called them).

I took one of the plain vanilla wafers and bit off a corner.

"I've never been to Kasungu," I said.

"You'd love it. Great game watching, there is a small lake outside the lodge and all the animals come down to drink at dusk. Elephant, buffalo, nyala."

That was a hint. I was not going to be coy. I needed to work on my audacious behavior.

Chapter 6

"I could get the jeep for a weekend." I offered. "Any interest in being my game scout?"

"You bring the binoculars and a bottle of wine and I'll consider it," she said with a smile.

"Done deal." I responded eagerly, knowing that the deal was just beginning.

Breakfast with Kamuzu

Banda in America

The historic path of young Hastings Banda deepened in the gold mines of South Africa after his epic march south. There, like all the African workers, he spent interminable hours deep in the earth - twelve, thirteen, fourteen hours a day. He lived in the slum of worker dorms. One shower per five hundred workers, and two toilets. There were no women or children there, only thousands upon thousands of dirt poor African men, sweating daily to extract ounce after ounce of wealth for the whites.

His ambition did not end in a dark hole in the earth, spading for gold. He rose to a clerk's position and extracted himself from the thankless mines. A white minister took young Banda under his wing, schooling him further until he completed the equivalent of eighth grade.

In South Africa, Banda joined the African Methodist Episcopal Church, an Ethiopian, black separatist church. He became devout and committed to the church's doctrine that black men should run their own affairs in Africa. He taught Sunday School for many years. At one of the church's annual conferences in the early 1920s, Banda presented a visiting American Bishop with a ceremonial lion-tail fly whisk. The Bishop agreed to underwrite Banda's further education.

The next stage of his journey was considerably farther from home. Hastings Banda left for America. He sailed on a freighter. Soon out of port he became violently sea-sick but improved by mid-Atlantic. When he saw the Manhattan skyline, it was like a vision of a future century. Kamuzu Banda arrived in New York City virtually penniless, although not without dreams.

Banda's early years in America were spent at the African Methodist Episcopal Church Institute in Ohio where he completed high school. Records show that he then attended the University of Indiana at Bloomington for two years. Banda then transferred to the University of Chicago in 1930 where he studied history and political science and was awarded a Bachelor of Philosophy degree the following year. While in Chicago, he contributed to some of the earliest linguistic studies of his native tongue, Chichewa.

He spent an extended period at Meharry Medical College in Tennessee, completing a medical degree at the historic black school. He was the first medical doctor from Nyasaland, no small accomplishment, no small testimony to his intellect and ambition. Yet, the New World was not his home, and he prepared to make his first step back across the Atlantic Ocean.

Perhaps equally significant to the educational achievements gained in America was the formation of Banda's racial views. During his twelve years in America, he experienced the worst and best in race relations.

In Tennessee he saw a black man lynched by a mob of angry whites in the light of burning crosses and hate-filled faces. Then again, the young African received the patronage of several wealthy whites and earned applause from all-white audiences who paid to hear a 'real African' talk about life at home.

These experiences resulted in Hastings Kamuzu Banda having a racial tolerance of noble degree. From then onward he preached a doctrine of racial tolerance. Yes, the black man should govern black Africa, but whites could also find a home there. Whites in the apartheid regimes were morally wrong, driven by fear and ignorance, but this weakness should be fought with cultural exchange and collaboration. Kamuzu favored non-violence in this idealistic phase of development.

Hastings Banda's return across the Atlantic was not directly to Mother Africa. His goal was to return as a medical missionary to his homeland in the Protectorate of Nyasaland as soon as possible. However, colonial requirements included medical certification in the United Kingdom. He left America for Edinburgh, Scotland, where he enrolled at the School of Medicine of the Royal College of Physicians and Surgeons in 1938, certain he was on his way back to Africa.

With his American degree in hand, he was far ahead of most students, and spent much of his time practicing his specialty under the supervision of some of the best surgeons of the time. It was not long before Banda was fully certified and ready to move on.

Unfortunately, several of the most blatant moments of racism ever to personally face Dr. Banda now surfaced and his dream of becoming a medical missionary was cruelly crushed. It happened first when he applied to work as a missionary surgeon in Nyasaland. The responding telexes announced that white nurses in the north refused to work under the black doctor and that he was not welcome.

When he tried to offer service to his home through the Colonial Office they hesitated. There was debate on whether he should be paid a salary equal to what white doctors earned; debate on whether he would be allowed to treat white patients; even debate about whether he would be allowed to swim in the recently built pool in Zomba with others in the Colonial Service.

Although clearly disappointed at this outcome, Banda did not turn bitter. He decided to stay in England for the time being and to practice the calling he loved so dearly, medicine. Dr. Banda then settled into the life of a practicing physician in a middle class London suburb. He practiced there for almost twenty years. From his patient's testimonials, he was a fine physician, who made house calls on cold winter nights.

Having succeeded in obtaining an advanced education with the help of many people, Dr. Banda intended to repay the debt with his own good deeds. Over a period of years during his life in London, he financed the education of over forty Africans, most but not all, from Nyasaland. Taking after the missionary fathers, he was stern. If a student lapsed, academically or morally, he or she was sent packing back to a hut in the bush without discussion.

Nearly forty years of age, he might have spent the rest of his life comfortably in England, practicing medicine and becoming wealthy. Medicine had been the professional love of his life but colonial politics was in the air and this became his new focus. He became one of the few educated Africans who responded to British plans.

Dr. Banda began to hear the government's plans for the amalgamation of several African colonies, including his homeland, Nyasaland. The statesman agreed, and remote colonists echoed their sentiments, that there would be greater efficiency, simpler administration, and shared benefits if the two Rhodesias and Nyasaland were combined.

But this was not at all how the Africans saw it. For Nyasaland, Dr. Banda recognized, being combined with the more powerful Rhodesias, would spell the absolute end of freedom, and it was this threat that caused him to ratchet up his political instincts.

There was exchange between the colonies and Great Britain. Among the expatriate luminaries gathered in England were Mohandas Gandhi of India, Juleous Nyerere of Tanganyika, Jomo Kenyatta of Kenya, and Dr. Hastings Kamuzu Banda of Nyasaland. They found each other. They talked, dreamed, planned and waited. For Dr. Banda it seemed he waited a lifetime, or two, but not quite an eternity.

World War II interrupted most of the evolving thought on the African colonies as the focus turned to defeating the axis powers. Banda himself refused to be enlisted on the grounds of conscientious objection. During these war years he gave alternative service within the Great Britain.

When the war ended, thoughts returned to consolidation of African colonies. In Britain, parliament organized the debate. Some argued that the pull of Southern Rhodesia, the strongest colony in Central Africa, would either be south, to a political alliance with South Africa, or to the north with the protectorates of Northern Rhodesia and Nyasaland. The preference was clearly for the northern alliance, particularly since South Africa was in the midst of institutionalizing a form of racism called apartheid.

There was also fear that the spreading idealism of the communists might sweep Central Africa up, crushing British hegemony. Finally, if Britain was indecisive, the black nationalist movements themselves would win the day.

The solution, taken with some degree of urgency, was to create the Central African Federation, a political unity of Nyasaland, Northern and Southern Rhodesia in 1953. Banda was devastated by the decision of his long adopted countrymen. All his efforts, and they had been extensive, failed to prevent Nyasaland from being swept up into the Central African Federation. In August 1953, with the indignity of the Federation finally imposed upon his homeland, Dr. Hastings Kamuzu Banda left England and moved south to the Gold Coast, the African staging point for his return to the Motherland.

Breakfast with Kamuzu

A Man with Good Power

The problem of a rock climbing partner was not easily solved. I tried teaming up with several expatriates but found myself frustrated. There was the no show problem with some of the young volunteers. "Sorry mate," Ian called me to say. "Too much bloody booze last night, can't make it today." That cut my Saturday adventure short on more than one occasion.

There was still one pioneering British climber living in the country by the name of Frank Kippax. The guidebook to Mount Mulanje listed several first ascent climbs by Kippax. We had spoken over the telephone and spent a lovely afternoon top-roping climbs in the Shire Highlands together. But Frank was almost sixty. He hadn't done serious climbing in over twenty years, so I valued his friendship but could not count on him as a partner for the West Face of Chambe Peak.

I had to think more creatively. Looking out a window into my garden, I noticed the tremendous progress my gardener had made. The yard, almost two acres, began with nothing but bare, red, laterite earth because the house was new and I was the first tenant. A year had passed.

Now the garden beds were established and the plants grew at a fevered pitch. My cactus and succulent garden had over forty species. Between the beds, a plush carpet of green grass, each blade planted one-by-one in the African fashion grew thickly. I had a line of seven foot tall acacias planted by the front driveway, and purple flowering jacarandas dispersed around the yard for shade.

As I sat pondering the climbing problem, the gardener, a young man named Cite (pronounced Sea-tay), short and muscular as a bull, toiled away energetically in the vegetable patch under a hot sun.

Just then an idea crossed my mind: Could Cite become my climbing partner? He was the hardest worker I had ever seen, never complaining, constant, spirited. The one big problem between us would be communication. I did not speak the local language, Chichewa, and Cite spoke only a little English. But climbers required only a limited vocabulary and we could construct this. More importantly, I needed someone with guts, someone with strength, someone I could trust with my life, who had time to go climbing. I rushed into the kitchen and spoke to Nelson, the wizened cook.

"Nelson."

"Yes bwana."

"I need a man to go mountain climbing with. The expats have all let me down. I need an African. Do you think Cite can do the job?"

"Bwana, that man, Cite, he is a good man, a hard worker, very strong. I think he can do the job."

"Call him in. You translate, please."

The small, smiling cook, whom had become like a grandfather to me, stepped out the back door and called Cite over. The young man put down the gardening tools and came running.

Nelson began a discourse in Chichewa. Cite listened carefully, consuming the cook's words deliberately. Then a big smile swept across his face, he nodded his head modestly and in halting English said to me, "I can try."

"Nelson, please tell Cite that this afternoon after lunch we are going up to Nkhoma Mountain and I will show him what I mean by mountain climbing."

The cook translated, using his own words and explanation, and Cite trotted off to ready himself.

Then Nelson turned to me and said, "Bwana, you have picked well. That Cite has good power."

"I believe you, Nelson," I said, assessing the idea even as my words came out. "I don't think I'll need the expatriate climbing partner anymore. Let's make this into a little Malawian-American enterprise."

Chapter 8

"Yes Bwana. That is very good," he said with a broad grin, excitement flooding his eyes. The cook stepped outside to the laundry machine in a quick shuffle, leaving me alone for a second.

As if remembering a sweet dream, I felt the happiness of an epiphany. It was an African mountain I desired, and it called for an African solution. Cite was not just a pick-up off the street, he was the right man to join me. He was a free being. I could train him completely. Suddenly, the warm joy of possibility filled me, African joy.

Nkhoma Mountain sprouted out of the plains like a giant termite mound with fluted ridges ambling down from top to bottom. The first climbing lesson for Cite was a simple bouldering session, a brief romp on the huge rocks that had rolled off the mountain.

I wanted to show him some of the gear, so I brought *rock climbing shoes*, a *climbing rope*, and the protective equipment called chocks, which fit into the crack to protect the lead climber in case of a fall.

We took off from the house by foot and hiked a good hour until I found the material I needed, a fifteen foot boulder. There wasn't much use in trying to explain climbing to him, since we didn't speak the same language, so I put on my shoes and faced the problem.

This was second nature for me, but as I grasped two holds on the boulder face and stepped onto the rock with my climbing shoes, Cite must have thought I was insane. Like a spider, I meticulously moved up the rock until I reached and pulled over the top. I came down to where Cite was standing and pointed to the rock indicating that he give it a try.

He took to the face without shoes. He was almost a foot shorter than I. It was a huge struggle for him to match my moves because of our height difference but he persevered, leaving a bit of flesh on the rock before pulling over the top successfully. I watched his effort and was impressed. When he came around to where I stood, I shook his hand and congratulated him. The partnership was sealed.

I had brought an extra harness and pair of rock climbing shoes to Africa, on the lark that I might find someone to fit in them. I pulled them out of my pack and handed them to Cite. His eyes lit up and a big smile filled his face. He slipped into the shoes and *climbing harness* and I taught him climbing knots such as a bowline, double-fisherman's and water knot. We spent the rest of the day practicing with the climbing gear and rope.

Those who said the Africans couldn't do it, and there were many expatriates who said so, no matter what the 'it' was, were going to eat crow. I was going to teach this man to be a skilled rock climber and together, if it was within our reach, we were going to attempt the unclimbed West Face of Chambe Peak, Malawi.

The Gold Coast

Dr. Hastings Kamuzu Banda returned to Africa via the Gold Coast, a relatively wealthy colony on the west coast, where power was shifting into the hands of the Africans. Money was an issue and for a while Dr. Banda quietly continued his profession as a medical doctor, avoiding the limelight of politics in the Central African Federation.

Communications with his homeland were difficult, but reports trickled in, telling him of the indignities Nyasaland was incurring as part of the Central African Federation. It was just as Banda had predicted all along. Nyasaland's interests were being submerged to those of The Federation. The influence of Southern and Northern Rhodesia grew as more resources were extracted there. Just as stalled development and a poor resource base made Nyasaland's shrink.

Even more significant than the economic disparities was the far stronger control and influence of white colonists in the Rhodesias as compared to Nyasaland. As the vocal corps of white colonialists had their say, a brand of penetrating racism took control and tainted everyday life. Banda once said that in Rhodesia when a white man passed him on a sidewalk, he was compelled to move out of his path. He was not allowed to sit next to a white person while trying on a pair of shoes.

In 1957 one event clearly influenced Banda to return to his homeland. While still living in the Gold Coast he witnessed the country's establishment as the first former colony to become an independent black nation in Africa and the changing of the name to Ghana. It was the start of decolonization across the continent, but the sting of Federation with the Rhodesias sent just the opposite message to the people of Nyasaland.

Nyasaland politicians began to court Banda with letters and personal visits to Ghana but he resisted a hasty return. To fight the Federation and gain sovereignty, they implored, Nyasaland needed an educated, senior, internationally known figure who could convince the British that adequate leadership existed to set the country free. No one fit that description better than Dr. Hastings Kamuzu Banda.

Ants in the Tree

Stepping through the cultural looking glass, foreigners may be quick to judge, prone to misinterpret, and apt to misuse. I found this out over lunch at the very start of flying ant season.

Flying ants are one stage in the life of African termites. It is their most rapid mode of dispersal. At the end of the dry season, when the first rains come, out of giant, red termite mounds burst droves of winged termites throughout the effected lands. Not just a few hundred, but thousands upon tens of thousands, upon millions, in just a few hours. The wings are delicate as snow flakes, and if you sit behind glass, on the night of the first rain, looking outside into a lighted area, you may think it is snowing. A blizzard of living insects fills the air.

Far from being a plague upon the Africans, the flying ants are a moving feast. Cooking them is not required. Simply pluck a live one from the sky, grab the succulent body, pull off the wings, and toss the wriggling corpus into your mouth. Chew, swallow and enjoy.

People of all sorts come out to enjoy the free meal. Businessmen in suits, security guards in green uniforms, women in bright *chitenje*, small, naked children. It is not done hurriedly but calmly, deliberately, in moderation. There is more than enough for all to indulge. It does not last long, the abundant gift from the earth; a few hours, a night, half a day at a time. There may be a few waves at the start of the rains but fewer as the season moves on.

Some restaurants offer a dish called "Ants in the Tree." In this recipe the "ants" consist of ground beef, chopped onions, and a touch of tomato sauteed in oil. The "tree" will be large fan-like leaves of lettuce. Drop a spoon full of "ants" into a "tree," roll the lettuce leaf closed and voila, you have a portion of "Ants in the Tree." It is a popular dish in Lilongwe restaurants.

Spurred by the seasonal outburst of flying ants and my knowledge of the ants in the tree recipe, I asked Nelson if he could prepare a hybrid dish for lunch. He was more than amenable and I looked forward to the meal.

When I came home at noon, it was a typical day in the early rains, a sprinkle the night before released a myriad of flying ants and Nelson had collected a small basket full, easily kept alive overnight. By noon only scattered black clouds hung in the blue sky like promising fruits. The temperature was hot. Karen joined me for lunch.

We sat at a round wooden table, inside the screened-in porch, surrounded by my profuse garden. Small, colorful birds fed on the nectar of orange flowers growing off tall aloe stalks.

"Beautiful birds," Karen said, noticing a pair of tiny sunbirds with bright yellow breasts, iridescent green heads and backs. Their wings moved so rapidly that they were invisible even as the birds hovered, poking their small, sharp bills into the base of flowers. "What are they?"

"Sunbirds," I replied, "collared sunbirds. They play the same ecological role as hummingbirds do back home." I had *The Birds of Malawi* which was not illustrated but I cross-referenced its entries with the photographs in *Robert's Birds of Southern Africa*. The sunbirds were relatively easy to identify, especially at close proximity.

"What's for lunch?" she asked, "I always look forward to Nelson's cooking."

I was waiting for that question. "Today we have a special treat, guess."

"Fresh chambo?" she fathomed. Chambo was the most delicate of lake fishes, coveted by all.

"Wrong, guess again."

"Lamb, I heard there was some home raised lamb at Nkhoma Mission. I bet it's lamb."

"Wrong."

"I give up."

"Today we are featuring 'Ants in the Tree'" I said cheerily, "with the real thing; fresh caught flying ants instead of ground beef."

"You're kidding," she said, her thin, beautiful, red lips moving from an enticing smile to a frown of grave skepticism.

"The termites have been cooked, they won't wriggle," I said, trying to be convincing.

"I'm not interested," she said curtly.

Fortunately, I had a back-up plan. "Nelson wasn't sure you'd be thrilled with the bugs, he's made a salad as well."

"Thank goodness someone has sense," she added, a noticeable look of relief crossing onto her pretty face.

No sooner had I explained the menu than the cook appeared with a tray full of goodies. A large, wooden salad bowl full of shredded lettuce, red onion, avocado, tomato and cucumber, all grown in the garden, stood out prominently. Two wooden serving spoons with zebra heads carved into the tops of the handles rose above the bowel. A small pouring cup held the cook's homemade vinaigrette dressing.

In another bowl, large well-washed lettuce leaves, the "trees," were stacked up invitingly. In a smaller glass dish, transparent for effect, Nelson piled the main course - the "ants." Inside this bowl rested a dark mass of thin, cylindrical bodies, individually about pinky-finger sized, interspersed with small, transparent, cubed onions and bits of tomato. Of course, the lacy wings had been removed. The abundant grease, a combination of cooking lard and the arthropodal exudate floated everywhere like unfossilized amber.

"Um, um, um," I could not help but add sardonically. "Thank you Nelson, it looks great."

"Bwana will like," he said, smiling from ear to ear in just pride. "And madam?"

"No thank you Nelson. Just salad, please."

Nelson set the tray down and placed each item onto the table.

"Thank you Nelson," I said, finally habituated to the constant politeness of my staff. I was returning the same in-kind.

The cook stepped back inside the house, leaving us alone.

"May I serve you some salad madam?" I asked, trying to be comical.

"Please bwana," replied Karen with a charming smile again gracing her thin, smooth-skinned face.

I took up the servers, gripping them just below the zebra heads and hefted a generous portion of salad onto her plate. She poured some rich, purple vinaigrette dressing on top.

"Now for the main event," I said in anticipation.

"Your main event," Karen said.

I selected one of the thick hand-sized lettuce leaves for the tree which would hold my coveted ants and put it squarely in the middle of my plate.

I plunged a large steel spoon it into the bowl of termite bodies and came out with about a dozen. Orange oil dripped off the spoon and across the table. I placed the first dollop into the lettuce leaf. Thrice more I spooned the ant protein into the tree, making myself a generous pocket full of ants in the tree - a la Nelson. It was our special recipe, unique to the household, prepared just the way I requested. I rolled the leaf shut and without further fanfare greedily snapped off a bite.

There simply was no other face to make in the presence of a woman I wanted to impress than one of sheer enjoyment. The taste was rich and nutty, enhanced by the blending of onion, tomato and salt into the fried insects. The plump, juicy bodies felt like fingers of liver when I bit down onto them. Altogether not bad, I thought, and I proceeded to happily munch down the first helping of ants in the tree.

Our conversation was minimal. There seemed to be more than enough going on with the meal itself, the nearby sunbirds and the perfect clarity of the African sky, now empty of clouds.

Relishing the rich delicacy of my own version of ants in the tree, I could not stop myself before eating a full five portions. Karen was more lady-like in her salad consumption.

Nelson served fresh fruit and steaming coffee to complete the meal. Karen's driver appeared and another typical lunchtime in Malawi ended. I walked her to the car and gave her a peck on the cheek.

"Next weekend to Kasungu?" she asked.

"Yes, I'll drive."

Not long after she left, I felt the heaviness of the rich meal ball up in my stomach. I began burping up the florid air of greasy, fried termites and pretty soon I found myself heaving the entire ants in a tree meal into the toilet. I vomited until my stomach almost turned inside out and my head throbbed like the worst hangover. Upon introspection, I had badly misused the manna of the flying ants of Malawi. Would I misjudge the continent's longest rock climb so badly? That remained to be seen.

Breakfast with Kamuzu

Return

Swooping down from the sky like a white-headed fish eagle, the plane landed on a tarmac runway in Blantyre to an airfield surrounded by hopeful Africans. On-board was one of their own people, a man who had lived in distant places for more than forty years, a great healer, a protector, the great savior or *Ngwazi*, returning to Nyasaland just when his people needed him the most.

Dr. Hastings Kamuzu Banda stepped out of the aluminum-winged bird to a loud cry from a people he had not seen or heard in almost a lifetime. The white policemen restrained the crowd with billy clubs, preventing a riot of enthusiasm from spilling onto the airstrip. A government car quickly swept Dr. Banda up and took him straight to colonial, now Federation, headquarters in Zomba. There he came face-to-face with his nemesis, the Federation-placed Governor.

Once inside the wood-paneled office, the two men shook hands politely but eyed each other skeptically. Then the Englishman addressed the African.

"Dr. Banda," he said in a cold, objective tone, "you are welcome back to your homeland." A pregnant pause ensued before the grey-haired man added, "so long as you behave yourself. And that means there can be no agitation," he warned sternly. "The course of events has already been determined."

"Mr. governor," replied the unintimidated Banda, "the winds of change blow far and wide across Africa." A slight smile escaped from the doctor's reserve and he added, "I am only one of those slight breezes."

Indeed, he was a small man. Almost, if not exactly, sixty years of age in this year of his return, 1958. The governor expected a more complacent response. He was not used to an African standing up to his threats.

"Banda," said the governor with consternation in his voice, "this is not London. Here your kind knows their place."

Banda interrupted, "this is **our** place."

The governor grew angry and screamed. "This is the Central African Federation, a part of it anyway, and there is nothing you can do to change that!"

Keeping his face expressionless, Kamuzu Banda only replied, "it is good to be back home."

"I'm sure," said the governor, lowering his voice, "now go and tend your garden, take a wife or two, but for God sakes, no politics."

At that point the governor was through with his interview. He called into the hallway, "Aide! Assist Dr. Banda into town." Then the governor looked once more at the small African man dressed in London finery and said to him, "Dismissed."

Wildfire

Everyday life in Africa is full of raw tragedy. Life is more precarious. Women die in childbirth. Infant and childhood mortality takes two of five new lives. Malarial fever burns up brains. My home at the base of Nkhoma Mountain was surrounded by bush, and disaster was never far away.

Dreaming of a big meal, a little boy named Savimbi took up his stick and walked towards the orange blaze. The fire cut through the dry grass with a sharp crack. Flames rose into the tall bushes, towering above him like a cobra. An evil black smoke curled behind Savimbi as he ran ahead of the mayhem searching for fleeing rodents.

Poor Savimbi, his little tummy groaned with hunger. There had been almost no food in the village for almost a month. Maize was the staple; it was ground into flour and mixed with boiling water until a sticky blob came out from the cooking pot. There were times when his mother made this type of grits twice a day. Then meals dwindled to once a day, and lately, he had not seen such abundance in a week.

With the maize scarce, they scraped wild roots out of the earth and ate bitter nuts off baobab trees. Even these were rare in a family of seven children, two parents, a grandmother, and many cousins. The grass fires were an important hunting ground, an opportunity to supplement the meager diet with protein. How he had fooled those other boys who went off fishing.

Suddenly, a mouse broke away from a dark clump of grass and scampered towards a bush. The keen-eyed boy stepped stealthily ahead of the mouse. He lowered the club to knee height and watched the shadow of the stick track the small creature like a hawk in the sky.

Savimbi beat the club down on the tiny mouse skull, stunning the creature. One more flick of the wrist and its life was completely drained. The boy quickly picked up the morsel of grey fur by its spindly tail and dropped it into a small bag, hanging from a leather thong, around his shoulder.

The blaze raced on erratically. Other predators, the multicolored lilacbreasted rollers, iridescent with thick black whiskers, kestrels, a sleek black mongoose, and a few scraggly village dogs, watched hungrily as the flight of lesser creatures continued ahead of the bush fire.

For a moment Savimbi doubled back behind the flames to the carpet of black and grey ashes. Here it was eerily silent, the smoking earth stood still and bare. His callused feet felt the hot, soft, powdery remains.

At the head of the fire he saw the dogs jumping wildly. He thought a nest of mice had been flushed and moved out in front of the flames again. Three dogs chased a hare, racing far off into a field after the hapless prey.

In better times the boy would have joined the pack, even fought the dogs for the meal. Today he was too weak and could only watch as the circle of canines descended on and tore into the hare. Standing powerless to challenge the dogs, his belly stood out, an empty growling pot. His bony arms hung limply at his sides, and his orange, curly hair filled with ash.

The wind picked up, gusting irregularly and unpredictably switching direction. It turned the fire towards a thick stand of woods.

Savimbi then saw a large brown mouse, confused by the wind, sitting motionless on an island of rock. He crouched low and began stalking. At the same time a black crow dove at the mouse, missing but sending it racing towards the cover of the woods. Savimbi cursed the bird. It rose skyward and landed effortlessly on a tree branch, then looked down mockingly at him.

The boy plunged into the woods in pursuit of the mouse. His hunger, the black mist, the snarling flames all exaggerated the size of the mouse to something greater than it was. In his mind, it grew larger than the hare, larger than a duiker, to the size of a bush pig, enough to feed the whole family. Hunting the little brown mouse became his entire focus.

Thinking he saw a mousy shape scurry ahead, the small boy continued deeper into the woods. Thrashing through thornbush he cut himself, bled and scraped an eye. Choking smoke filled the tangled woodland and Savimbi tripped over a log, twisting his ankle and knocking his head. Desperately, he began crawling on all fours. Then he heard the coming of the flames, a roar as final as that of a lion.

Breakfast with Kamuzu

The Matter

Planning and training for the first ascent of Chambe Peak distracted me from duties at the Ministry of Health. Fortunately, the staff had grown into a team and I was operating with absolute faith in them. The project seemed to be running smoothly. That is, until I arrived one afternoon to a query from my secretary, Jane.

"The bank has called," she relayed, "the manager says that he has a check with your signature on it but it doesn't look like your handwriting."

"How much is it for?"

"Twelve-hundred kwacha," she said, about five-hundred U.S. dollars. "I told Hexy. He said not to bother you."

"Where is he?"

"He went down to clear up the matter."

At that moment, my trust sank to river bottom. I knew I needed to beat him to the bank.

"What kind of transport does he have?"

"He's going by foot."

"Get Viswell, I've got to arrive there first."

Jane stepped out the door to get the driver. I called the bank and told them that if Hexy arrived to stall him. I would be there momentarily.

Now the cogs were churning. Hexy was the administrator. He kept the books and prepared all the payroll and expense checks. I was the only one with signatory power. He brought the checks to me to be signed, and he reconciled everything coming back from the bank. It was possible, even likely, that some kind of funny business was going on and I was going to find out.

I trotted out the door and found Viswell already cranking the engine.

"Hurry," I screamed, "to the bank." We sped away down the thin, crowded streets of Lilongwe. It was only a ten minute drive, but it would be a good forty minute walk. At the bank, I jumped out, perspiring now in a most offensive way, and dashed inside.

The Bank Manager, Mr. Gondwe, was waiting for me just inside the front door.

"Has Hexy been here yet?" I asked.

"No sir."

"Good, let's see that check."

I was ushered behind a low, wooden, swinging, counter-top door and into a back room. The check sat on top of a cleared desk. One look and I knew it wasn't my handwriting. It was made out in pencil to an "H. Temba" and signed with my name.

"Forged," I exclaimed, "no doubt about it."

There was the question and the answer, exposed on that little rectangle of paper. It was a scam. The realization sent a shiver down my spine.

"If Hexy shows up, send him back to the office, okay?" I barked.

"Most certainly," replied Mr. Gondwe.

"And don't tip him off."

"Yes, sir."

I took the check with me. Back at the office I immediately went to the safe where the checkbook, stubs and canceled checks were kept. A quick review showed three other checks with the same forged signature. These had been made out to recognizable vendors, and it might have passed unnoticed except for the faintly visible erasure marks which showed the administrator's name on the payee section.

"Jane," I called. "Notify the police and the embassy, and if Hexy shows up, be prepared for a little action."

"Yes sir."

Viswell came into the office.

"Bwana," he said, "this is very bad."

"I know that Viswell."

"Bwana, not just for that criminal, but for you."

"It's only money," I stammered.

50

Chapter 13

"Bwana, the problem for you is worse."

"What on earth do you mean?"

"Sometimes, these criminals, if they know that you have found out, they, well, they can be very bad."

"Hexy's already been very bad. What do you mean?"

"I mean, he can call his friends and they will kill you."

"Me! I didn't do anything."

"You know too much, bwana. Be careful."

Great, I thought, I've uncovered a theft and I'm on death row.

"Thanks Viswell, I appreciate your concern."

Hexy never showed up at the office that day or the next. That night as I lay in bed thinking about the day's dramatic events, a black cat suddenly appeared at the window, lifting its tail like a squirming snake and hissing loudly. It stared me right in the eyes before loudly scratching the glass with a paw and running off into darkness. How it got inside the gate, past the guard and onto my window sill, I'll never know, but the dark omen left me shaking in the night.

Breakfast with Kamuzu

Clocktower Incident

Kamuzu Banda's return to Nyasaland was not without certain conditions to which his African brethren agreed. He was to be the president of the newly formed Malawi Congress Party, and all the various nationalist factions were to unite under this single entity. Banda alone had total authority to appoint board members. As the mouthpiece of the Malawi Congress Party and the people, he quickly set out on a tour of the country. His provocative speeches outlined the injustices they lived under in the Federation system but discouraged racism and violence. He emphasized the need for education and universal suffrage for the African population.

Curiously, these speeches were given in English, not because he had completely forgotten his native Chichewa, although he was rusty and his syntax archaic, but carefully in line with the traditional oratory style of Chewa chiefs who always spoke to villagers through an intermediary.

Banda still dressed as an Englishman, and his European appearance and manners, far from undermining him with his people, lent credibility to his efforts at uprooting an evil he knew from worldly experience. He traveled from Karonga in the north to Nsanje in the south. He spoke at lakeside villages such as Mangoche and Nkhata Bay.

His speeches were wildly successful, whipping up the enthusiasms of his audience to a frenzy and gaining him authority. In one case, the spill-over from a Banda speech caused what became known as the infamous Clocktower Incident in Blantyre.

The Clocktower is a familiar monument on the outskirts of Blantyre town, a prominent brick-laid tower with a large clock in it, used by all. After one particularly riveting speech in nearby Limbe, in which Dr. Banda appealed for racial cooperation, the crowd of Africans and speaker disbanded without trouble.

Many from the assembly then walked to a bus stop near the Clocktower. It was a Sunday, buses were infrequent and the crowd became impatient and rowdy. A few started throwing stones at passing cars with whites inside. In ten minutes of chaos, two European women were slightly injured and minor vandalism occurred.

The police responded, batons and shields drawn, but they could not proceed to actively disperse the crowd until the Riot Act was, literally, read aloud to the people. The officer on duty, unfortunately, could not produce a copy of this written statement and it was never read. Perhaps this small bureaucratic blunder spared what might have become a bloody, violent incident. Before anything further happened the crowd melted away.

Nonetheless, the Clocktower Incident was born. Next day the settler-run newspaper headline led with the bolded words "Mob Violence in Blantyre," and the story proceeded to condemn the African crowd, its leader Dr. Banda, and the response by the Federation government. The Clocktower Incident was the beginning of the end of cooperation between those ruling the Central African Federation, the white European colonists and the Africans of Nyasaland.

Potato Rock

The air was thick with dust from the burning fields and the sweltering heat. I talked Bruce, the only expatriate who ever came climbing with me, into making a roped ascent of Potato Rock, a small, free-standing landmark near Dedza.

I climbed first. He reluctantly followed. At one point he fell and I held the rope tight taking his weight. He dangled for a moment, regained his hold and then scraped upwards with a surge of adrenalin. When he joined me on the summit of Potato Rock, the heat really hit us and we sat down for a rest.

There was a fine view from the top. Africa was out there, two countries worth. To the south rose Dedza Mountain, covered in dark green pine forest. The trees grew in orderly rows, for miles upon miles, creating a softness to the eyes. The reserve was originally planted when Malawi was Nyasaland, under British colonial rule. It was an orderly British forest, and the Malawians had done a good job in keeping it so.

The road in front of us marked the border between Malawi and Mozambique. There were many villages sprinkled on the Malawian side of the road. These villages had a common design, a ring of huts around an open square. The houses were built of stick frames with mud plaster and thatched roofs.

Around each village were small plots, where brown corn stubble lay from the previous harvest, or blackened remains if the patch had already been burned. At this time of year Africa was set on fire in an attempt to return some fertility to the earth for next year's planting.

There were many people about. Boys herding flocks of cattle or goats. Women carrying laundry, clay pots filled with water, or baskets of white corn flour on their heads. They walked in single file lines. Men rode on bicycles with loads of firewood or goats tied out flat, on racks, over the back tires. Packs of children played by a slow winding creek. People scurried in and out of an open air market. Malawi was vibrant, busy, almost

55

chaotic with activity. Across the road, to the west, was Mozambique and a different story.

Mozambique was a ghost town compared to Malawi, a vast uncultivated stretch of bush. I looked whimsically at a few distant plugs of granite; rock I longed to climb but knew were forbidden to visit. There were armed rebels hiding out there. They crossed the border at night and raided villages, stealing food, clothing, hardware, animals and even women.

"Soldier's things," they said, "materials needed to fuel the democratic opposition." But no one thought of them as freedom fighters any more, just bandits - dirty, ruthless anarchists.

The civil war shut down this part of Mozambique, in fact, most of Mozambique inside the coast. People fled for their lives, sometimes in the middle of the night. They were burned out of villages, away from their already meager plots of land. They took only what could be carried on their heads or backs, or led by tethers, or piled in ox carts if they were rich enough to own one. More than a million Mozambicans were refugees, more than half a million in Malawi alone.

To the south we saw the refugee camps on the Malawi side of the border. They were similar to the Malawian villages but on a larger, more congested scale. Thousands of sagging, hastily built huts were clustered together in disorderly rural slums. Far away as we were, we could still see a mass of people gathered together for a food distribution by the Red Cross.

We took in this view silently, until the heat and dryness became unbearable. Bruce spoke first. "Let's peel off this spud and drive into Dedza for a cold one at Randall's Bottle Store. You owe me one."

"How come I owe you one? I should be a hero for saving the life of an important American diplomat. Your fall could have provoked an international incident," I said with a smirk. It was true, Bruce was a high ranking diplomat in the American Embassy, although it was hardly a case of heroism on my part.

Chapter 15

"You owe me one because if I died I'd come back to kill you for dragging me half way up this rock and then dropping me. It's your good fortune that I survived. That's worth at least one Green," he said, with that twist of logic only diplomats and used car salesmen possess.

Sure enough, a Green, the vernacular for a Carlsberg lager, was a small price to pay for his magnanimous effort on the rock.

"There's just one little matter separating us from the beers," I mentioned casually.

"What's that?" said Bruce.

"There's no place to anchor the rope up here," I pointed out, casting a disappointed glance across the smooth, flat summit. "I guess we better call for a rescue."

"There's only one helicopter in the country, and you know who owns that."

"The Life President," I said. "I thought you were close with him?"

"Sure, but I forgot my cellular hot line."

"Okay, I've got another idea." I proceeded to explain to him a technique used in the Needles of South Dakota. We rehearsed our roles and took action.

Keeping myself glued to the flat summit by virtue of friction alone, I gingerly lowered Bruce to the ground. He then anchored his end of the rope to a tree. I pulled the free end of the rope tight against the anchor and threw the loose end off the opposite side of the rock. Then I slid down the rope, rappelling in the usual method used by climbers. It was a successful, somewhat ingenious solution to the problem of being stuck on top of a rock pinnacle. I walked around the rock to where Bruce was waiting.

"That was fun," he said, facetiously.

I pulled and coiled the rope .We walked back to the car and drove south towards the town of Dedza.

"Will we get a beer at the bottle store?" I asked, hopeful that today would be an exception to the usual lack of everything in Africa.

"Yup," he said, swerving around a red ox-drawn cart.

"A cold one, even a slightly cool one would be a miracle," I said. "Any chance of that?"

"Yup," he said, bouncing the Peugeot in and out of deep pot holes. "You'll get an ice cold beer, as long as there's power in Dedza. You'll like the bar, it's right out of a Graham Greene novel," he said with a sly grin. He signaled and turned off the main road into Dedza.

"If we're lucky Major Ross will be there."

"Who's Major Ross?"

"He was a Major in Her Majesty's service in World War II. He commanded a platoon of Nyasas in Burma. After the war he returned to Malawi and recruited Malawians for the mines in South Africa. He retired and lives in Dedza. The Major knows everything about everyone. He's a great source of intelligence, especially on the Mozambican civil war. He's a regular at Randall's and a good friend of mine."

African Poet

The hamlet of Dedza consisted of two rows of adobe buildings lining the unpaved street. It reminded me of the Main Street in a wild west town, a hundred years ago. There were hitching posts but for mostly oxen and goats. Horses didn't do well in this climate, disease knocked them all off, although a few managed to survive at Dedza's higher elevation.

The stores were basic - a trading post, a grocery store, several bars. The town appeared to be functional, although perhaps not functioning completely. We pulled in front of a building where a small sign advertised Randall's Rainbow Bottle Store. Its small, crooked door was painted green and had a crooked window next to it.

Bruce walked in with the confidence of a local. I was less sure of the endeavor. Inside was a narrow room with two square tables. The table to the left was occupied, while the one to the right sat empty. Ahead was a small rectangular opening where a man stood cramped in a tiny cubicle. That was the bar, without enough counter space to slide a glass down.

At one table sat an older Malawian man and a younger woman. The old man was dapper, with a pinstriped suit coat and almost matching pants. He had grey peppercorn hair and was clean shaven. He was drinking an orange Fanta.

The woman held a Coke with both hands. She wore a pink skirt and a red blouse with frills along the shoulders. Her Afro-style hair stuck out an inch or two longer than most women's in the country, and she had a red comb stuck in it. She had a large chest and her brassiere strained to be free of the blouse. She sucked her Coke slowly, wiggling her pink tongue inside the bottle's neck.

I ordered two Greens. The skinny bartender turned to a bright red Coke refrigerator, a vintage model. He lifted the silver door. A full stack of sweating Greens, Browns, and Golds, all versions of Carlsberg's best brews, waited inside. He pulled out two Greens, snapped off the caps and pushed the bottles our way.

I handed over two kwacha. We heard chatter in the room behind the bar.

A small passage led around the side of the bar, into another room. Here the roof extended out for about eight feet, to a wide cement railing. Further back was an open courtyard with two doors marked as the toilets at the far end.

We stepped into the room and the middle of a conversation. A few sentences whisked past us before we were noticed, then a cry arose from a seated white man.

"Bruce," a man called in a strong British accent. "Is that Bruce?" The old man cocked his head like a Loerie bird and addressed my friend again. "I say, it is Bruce. Have a seat."

A pair of bloodshot eyes glared up at us in half recognition. It was actually quite hard to be uncertain about Bruce. He was well over six foot tall, thin, with sandy hair, sea blue eyes and the sharp, serious features of a U.S. Naval Academy graduate. There weren't many like him in Malawi.

"Yes, Major Ross," said Bruce. "It's me."

"Oh, I say, it is you Bruce. Isn't it? Jolly good to see you. Come join us," said the inimitable Major Ross.

The Major was seated on a wooden bench, just under the rear window of the bar. His legs were crossed and he leaned over a dark wooden cane. He wore a three-piece woolen suit, a crisply pressed white shirt, and a black and red tie with a silver clasp. A white handkerchief stood at attention in his breast pocket. In one hand rested a glass half full of lacquer brown liquid.

Bruce made an effort to introduce me. "Major, this is my friend Glen."

For a white man, he was looking rather flushed, but he sat regally, for his condition. He was round, but not fat and bald.

There was a young Malawian man sitting to one side of the Major. It seems, from the two or three sentences we heard, that the young man was on the receiving end of a reminiscence about a commando raid near the Manipur Hills, in Burma, forty-three years ago. The young man seemed unperturbed at our arrival and the passing of the story.

Further down the bench from the Major was another European. He was the owner of the bar, Haynes Randall, now propped up against the wall, oblivious to all. His eyes were nearly turned up into his head. He was a rather Humpty Dumpty looking fellow, who was rolling about as if he might just fall off his fence and crack. His round jowls were as red as the Coke refrigerator.

For better or worse, this was a typical Saturday afternoon in Dedza. It was time to get stinking drunk. Bruce and I sat along the cement railing and began sipping our beers. The conversation turned towards Bruce.

"I say, Bruce old chap," said the Major, "I received a visit from that military attache of yours the other day. What's his name, Colonel Futz?"

"No, starts with a 'B'" corrected Bruce.

"Not a very discreet fellow. Seems he was found snooping around a village, on this side of the border, searching for an arms stockpile. Chaps found him poking around a chicken coop. Came out all covered in manure. Bloody fool even dropped his pistol. A granny returned it."

"That's our man alright, a perfect example of military counter-intelligence," said Bruce, sarcastically.

During this small exchange another man silently entered the room. He was a tall, handsome African, about forty wearing pleated khaki pants and a tan button down shirt which was frayed but not torn. A pair of leather suspenders drew everything smartly together. His tall, black boots reached almost to his knees.

His face was distinctive. His aquiline nose stood out gracefully, his dark eyes searched the room thoroughly and intelligently. His sideburns and goatee were neatly manicured. He sat down inconspicuously in a chair to the side.

He was soon recognized by the Major, who said, "Good afternoon, Mr. Ernest de Barbados. What brings you to Dedza town?"

"Good afternoon Major, and to you, Mr. Haynes," said the African in a deep, resonant voice. He politely tipped and removed his hat, a canvas bush cap with a leather drawstring, used in many armies across Africa. "I have come to pay respects to an elder statesmen in a near-by village. Nothing more."

"What'll ya have?" slurred Haynes.

"A Fanta, please," replied Ernest de Barbados.

"A Fanta," said Haynes in disgust. "I thought you were more of a man than that." He was speaking angrily, then drew a sober breath and said, "This man is the most ruthless cutthroat on this or that side of the border. Don't let his nice talk fool you. He was, or is, a Mozambican soldier, and a very tough one."

Ernest de Barbados eyed him knowingly and let the banter go on for a minute before saying softly to us all. "I am not really this person. Not anymore. My heart has grown soft. It has been too long. I am retired."

Haynes' ramble went on, "Stories. This one has stories, great stories, war stories, soldier stories, and what other kinds of stories?" Then he looked Ernest de Barbados in the face, and with solemn disrespect said.

"But I've heard your stories a hundred times so bore someone else."

That is how I met Ernest de Barbados the African soldier and poet. As soon as the orange drink was brought out, and another round of Greens attended to, we fell back into conversations. Due to the seating arrangement, Ernest de Barbados happened to be at my focus. He had a look of wakefulness, of deliberation and refinement that was rare, rare indeed, anywhere in the world. I felt a stroke of luck put me next to him.

"Where are you from?" I asked him, quite innocently, since it was clear that he was not your ordinary Malawian.

"That is not a simple answer," he said, staring into the bottle of soda where a chain of bubbles came fizzing up along the sides. "I was born in Mozambique," he said, taking a sip of the drink before opening up further. "But home is also here." He spoke in a deep Shakespearean baritone. "My mother was Malawian. My father a Mozambican. The border means nothing to me."

"But, I'm afraid, dear Ernest, it means something to others," said the Major, pawing at our conversation. "It seems you are unwelcome on either soil," he added, intimating that he had some special knowledge of the man's circumstances. "You see, my dear, dear friends," continued the Major. "Our distinguished guest is thought to be a recruiter for the rebels. They say he has an uncanny eye for promising soldiers and a persuasive tongue to fetch them. The Malawi Officials take some interest in his activities over here. Don't they, Ernest?"

"Thank you, Major, for the compliments, but they are greatly overstated. As for the suspicions of the local government, I assure you they are unsubstantiated."

"Even at the request of a whip?" said the Major, sharply.

"I was only taken in for questioning," said the African, cautiously. "I take no responsibility for the fears of others," he added. "Perhaps you are correct, Major. Neither soil is now my sanctuary, but in another time."

I did not know if he meant in the past or in the future.

"At least I can travel unnoticed," continued Ernest. "I pity you, that your skin reveals you so brazenly," he laughed gently. "I can travel in shadows. I can be anywhere. I can speak English to you, Chichewa to my Malawian cousins, and Portuguese to all Mozambicans."

I was hypnotized by his words, his voice, his dignity. "You seem well schooled," I said, not meaning to be rude, just curious about how this man came to be. "Where did you get that?"

"The Portuguese," he said proudly. "They educated me. It was not a common thing. You see I am an *assimilato*, if the old colonial term can be used."

"What do you mean by that?" I had to ask.

"It is a long story that must begin when I was a small boy. In those days it was a rigid society, that I must say about the

Portuguese, and difficult for Africans to get ahead in. They did not promote Africans, and never prepared us for the eventual fall of colonialism. Even the British did a better job of that. Didn't they, Major?" asked Ernest, with a glimmer of sarcasm twinkling in his eyes.

"Perhaps," answered the Major, as he contemplatively swirled his scotch around and around his glass.

Ernest continued. "The Portuguese masters trained few of us in Western skills. Not even for the most mundane tasks; as a barber, a clerk, or to work a simple machine - hardly the pinnacles of professional life. It was difficult, nearly impossible for an African to learn these things in colonial Mozambique."

Ernest de Barbados explained this bygone chronicle with the confidence of a history professor. I was spellbound. He went on.

"There was only one way to advance in the Portuguese system and that was to become, to be invited to become, an *assimilato*." He hesitated, sipping at his soda. "You ask me, I see the question in your eyes: What is an *assimilato*?"

"Our family lived in a small village near a military base. We were poor, but no more poor than our neighbors. My father farmed. He sold extra fruits and vegetables to the cook on the base. I delivered them to the compound under stern orders to neither lose, consume or sell any before reaching the kitchen."

"One day the cook looked down at me and said, 'Boy, do you want to become a man?'

'Yes, yes, of course father,' I said.

'Well then, serve this food out to the soldiers.'"

"I was a little frightened, but I wanted to do as he said. So it began. When I first I brought food to the soldier's tables, they laughed at me and tried to make me drop the tray. I dared not talk back and wouldn't give in to their taunts. I served the food and ran back into the kitchen The cook was amused and invited me to return the next day. As time went on the soldiers took an interest in me. They offered to let me go to school and learn proper Portuguese, something I never could have hoped for."

"When I was of age, they offered to let me become a soldier. It was a dream come true. But there is more to it than that because I had education. There were many other Africans in the army. They needed bodies. The uneducated were not treated as well as I. As an *assimilato* I had greater privileges. I ate in the mess with the Portuguese. I was paid on a higher scale, not quite equal to the Portuguese but considerably higher than my African brothers. Eventually, I was given an administrative job, and these were only given to Africans who were *assimilato*," he said with pride and paused to sip his drink. "That is all."

There was clearly a large part of the story left untold. That would be the war, the fighting between the Portuguese and the Africans, between Africans and Africans. The war began more than a decade ago and was still smoldering. The tables had turned. The Africans now ruled a socialist government in Maputo, the capitol city. It was the holdover Portuguese, white mercenaries and their African allies, who now lived secretly, on the run, in the bush, fighting a guerilla war.

I did not pursue these thoughts. They ran too near today. I did not want to hear him tell of the battles he had fought, how he had killed and tortured. But I knew he had been a fighting soldier, and that perhaps he still was. It was in his carriage, his strength, his silent walk.

Ernest de Barbados finished the last drops of his Fanta. His eyes scanned the room and everyone in it, finishing that too to the last drop. He was not at all nervous but it was clear that he had said his piece, and that other duties called him. Perhaps he was a recruiter for the rebels, and inwardly hoping one day to be on the winning side again, in an age when the *assimilato* would finally rule.

The ideological framework Ernest lived in was archaic. Colonialism, in its old form, was passe' and impossible to return to. Yet, there was something redeeming in Ernest de Barbados. It was partly the way he walked; silent, firm and proud. Partly how he dressed, in that crisp, clean, functional manner. And partly how he looked me straight in the eyes, without reluctance or rancor. I will never forget how he spoke, in that dramatic, poetical way, choosing words not just for convenience but effect.

Looking through the courtyard, I saw the sun turning another corner. Bruce and I still had an hour's drive back to our homes near the capital city. The road was dangerous after dark. We stood up to excuse ourselves.

The Major looked up and said. "Bruce, Bruce, I so enjoyed seeing you today. Next time, please, do stay for a meal."

Then the old soldier refocused his gaze on the young Malawian man, poured himself another shot of scotch whisky from a bottle resting at his feet and recommenced his explanation of the heroic Burmese campaign with the platoon of Nyasas he commanded, as though it had never been interrupted.

Ernest politely stood up to bid us farewell, cordially tipping his hat. As we walked outside the Rainbow Bar, the Major and Haynes and all the other characters faded into the evening shadows.

To where, to whom, to what fate Ernest de Barbados would be delivered, I knew I would never know. He was destined to become just another mystery in the great, dark continent of my mind. I did know that my happiness today came from living fully in Africa and having met one of her finest soldiers and poets.

Political Prisoner

Unrest grew in Nyasaland during 1959 and with rioting and vandalism increasing, the Federation brought in white police from Southern Rhodesia. This inflamed the people of Nyasaland and confirmed their belief that Nyasaland was to be a sub-colony of a white-ruled Central African Federation. Fifty-three Africans were killed in skirmishes. No whites died.

As Banda said upon his return, he would set the country on fire against the Federation, and tacitly more than overtly, that is exactly what his words did. The Federation proclaimed a State of Emergency and conducted Operation Sunrise, beginning with the arrest and detention of the African political leaders.

Kamuzu Banda was wearing pajamas when he was roused from bed by Special Forces and whisked away to Gwelo prison in Southern Rhodesia. Before long over one thousand Party members were in jails around Africa.

The Federation believed that incarcerating the political leaders would extinguish the movement. It temporarily quieted the flames but did not put them out. Meanwhile, as the leaders waited in jail cells, the more educated of them, Banda included, taught school to those less educated including lesson on the political and constitutional histories of Britain and America. Latin lessons became strategy meetings for the day when they would be set free.

The Nyasaland crisis reverberated far away in the halls of the British Parliament. An investigation was launched by a credible team to determine the veracity of reports. Their recommendations were selectively accepted, but concluded that the Federal response had been too extreme, illegal in its killings, and that a possible plot by the Africans to murder settlers was unsubstantiated (although there was some truth to the plans, they were never actualized).

After a period of relative quiet, the people throughout the country slowly began agitating again. Some political leaders were released and the British initially proposed constitutional change to bring about independence of the Federation as a unit. This was not well-received by the Africans and the British recognized if there were to be continuing relations with the freed nations, it would have to be as separate entities.

Those Nyasas not jailed rallied around Kamuzu Banda and made it clear that useful constitutional discussions could not take place while he was jailed. Incidents were beginning to take place again. The membership of the Malawi Congress Party grew from 8,000 to over 250,000 showing that popular support for change was real and grass roots. It became apparent that to avoid further crisis Banda would have to be freed.

Much like the night of his arrest, the jailers woke Kamuzu Banda up in his cell and secretly spirited him away, by night flight, back to Nyasaland. In Zomba the Governor himself handed Kamuzu Banda his release papers, setting his prisoner free after thirteen months of detention.

Tree Planting Day

Because of the failing rains, Tree Planting Day was held one month early, in December. This gave the trees a chance to spring roots, draw breath, and catch hold of the earth, with the hope of drinking in the earliest rains. There would still be a high mortality among young trees.

As an expatriate living in Malawi, I was encouraged to participate in Tree Planting Day. My students, organized by my counterpart Danny, were assigned to plant eucalyptus trees which I bought. These are not indigenous trees but ones often used for fuel wood because they grow rapidly and are easy to manage. At this time I had six available students in my office and we all met on the morning of the holiday.

I explained that four people would continue on a data entry assignment in the office while I would take the others over to Mphungu Primary School, not far from my house. We would only work a half day today. Cite had confirmed with the primary school principal that it was alright for us to bring the trees and plant them with the children.

When I asked for volunteers, my usually ambitious students were lukewarm about the idea. It came down to drawing straws, a game we all enjoyed, and Cosby and Wesley drew the short ends and got the job. The others remained in the air conditioned room, squinting over numbers and names.

The two students sat in the back seat. I was in the front seat next to Viswell. Cosby had worked in the ministry's accounting section, until the announcement came over the radio that he had been selected to go to the University of Malawi, in Zomba. He was temporarily retraining with me over the two week Christmas holiday. I was very fond of Cosby for several reasons.

No doubt my initial prejudice towards this young man was an irrational, emotional positive one. For Cosby Nkwazi, from Rumphi district in northern Malawi, Africa, was the spitting image of the American actor, Bill Cosby. I believe that this first struck me the moment he walked in the door for the first day of training, wearing a brown suit and patterned tie in a single Windsor Knot. But Cosby was not sent for training on the hopes that he would keep our office lively.

An aptitude test had been drawn up for all incoming students which involved the coding of a tricky question about village sanitation. Cosby answered with aplomb, was articulate and had good eyes, and so he became one of six persons selected out of the thirty for the advanced training course. And while Cosby only trained with me for two months that time, he gave creative, accurate work which pleased me.

Today Cosby spoke of his course load, and how he was planning on majoring in economics with a minor in computer science. It was, "A strong combination," I added. I asked him about the girls at school. He said now it was time for study, but he added, with a wry smile, that there was much beer at the University. He was very earnest.

Wesley, although older and having already completed a degree in Agriculture, was less talkative than Cosby. I saw him through the rear view mirror, head swaying back and forth like a cobra's, as he followed our conversation. In personality Wesley was as harmless as the giant millipedes which cross the roads in the rainy season. Soon we were parked in my driveway.

I pulled the wheelbarrow out of the garage and we filled it with the thirty wispy eucalyptus plants, potted in green plastic wrap the shape of tin cans. Cosby took the yellow three-wheeled raft and we walked up the dirt road towards the school. The street was filled with skipping, singing, African children, all wearing blue and white uniforms.

We were led to the principal's office, a bare room with a cement floor, iron sheet roof, one wide wooden desk, a few chairs, and many people standing about. I greeted them, and they reciprocated in rough unison. The principal was a round woman showing the signs of good health in the African way, wearing a head of hair more generously full than most.

70

They were expecting us. I spoke to madam principal, using stiff but clear English, explaining that I was an expatriate computer trainer and that my students and I were very grateful at being able to celebrate Tree Planing Day with the students and staff of Mphungu Primary School. These two men, I pointed to Cosby and Wesley, would stay behind to plant the trees. Then I left to attend to office duties.

Later that morning, Cosby and Wesley returned to the office, beaming with enthusiasm. I was surprised because I told them that as soon as they finished planting the trees they were free to go home. Of course, they knew this but had come anyway to tell me about the tree planting. I was anxious to hear what had happened.

Cosby proudly explained, "We were treated like VIP's," an expression well known in Malawi. "There was a ceremony and we sat in the seats of honor. There was dancing, and singing, and then we went to plant the trees in the schoolyard. The children dug the holes. We planted the trees. Then, after covering them with earth, we gave each tree a bucket of water to help them take root and grow."

Breakfast with Kamuzu

Towards Independence

In 1960, Britain's efforts at constitutional change within the Central African Federation met with deaf ears from its African constituency. The Federation leader's treatment of the disorders in Nyasaland were condemned in parliament and the brazen efforts of the Southern Rhodesians to police Nyasaland backfired.

Once freed from Gwelo jail, Kamuzu Banda reigned in his people, constantly reminding them of the four cornerstones of the Malawi Congress Party, "Unity, Loyalty, Discipline and Obedience." Before traveling to London to leverage his power, Banda reminded his leadership of the need to be exemplary during the struggle for independence.

The British government, meanwhile, was reshuffled through elections and sympathies changed. Finally, constitutional reforms acceptable to Banda were agreed to during the London meetings. Elections were planned in Nyasaland with a two-tier system of suffrage within the population based on educational attainment and income, resulting in the lower role containing mostly Africans and the upper mainly of Europeans. Two Councils would be formed out of the election and they would govern Nyasaland within the Federation context. Kamuzu returned to Nyasaland a hero.

The elections in Nyasaland occurred in August 1961 and the outcome was unambiguous. The Malawi Congress Party won a resounding victory and its President, Hastings Kamuzu Banda, took the unofficial reigns of power in Nyasaland.

The de facto result of elections was to squash the drive for an independent Federation and to get the British to agree in principle to a free and independent Nyasaland.

When the new Councils came to order, they immediately changed the face of the local and protectorate level government. Rules and regulations were modified to put more of the African in Nyasaland. It was a good start, everyone agreed, and the Councils worked productively through 1962. In effect, the Africans ruled.

Formal steps towards independence were taken in London at a constitutional conference in November 1962. By this plan the two Councils were converted to a Legislative Assembly and a Cabinet with the majority party's leader named Prime Minister. These constitutional changes came about in February 1963.

A final set of constitutional changes were agreed to in London in September 1963 with Dr. Banda. These modifications delivered universal adult suffrage, set the number of seats in the Assembly, and called for a general election in April 1964. Even more significantly, the British agreed that on the 6th of July, 1964, the historical protectorate of Nyasaland would withdraw from the Central African Federation and become the independent sovereign nation of Malawi. If the Malawi Congress Party was on the winning end of elections, Dr. Hastings Kamuzu Banda would become its first Prime Minister.

I asked my driver, Viswell, to stop by the United Nations office and pick Karen up before going to the market. I usually sent the cook with Viswell to shop for fresh foods, but today I wanted to buy gifts to send back home. Karen was an expert shopper.

A guard waved us through the checkpoint at the U.N complex. Karen was waiting just outside the front door, wearing a blue pleated skirt and white blouse with a rose pinned to her chest pocket. Viswell stopped the jeep, got out, and opened the door for her. She stepped up and into the back seat where I was sitting. I smelled the sweet aroma of the rose as we greeted each other with kisses on both cheeks. Viswell drove off.

"How exciting," she said, "that you're actually going shopping."

"It's the best way to prove I'm alive to the folks back home."

"Helps the local economy too."

Lilongwe is a small town and in a few minutes we were parked in the dirt lot next to the market. It was crowded. The main bus station in Old Town was nearby.

"Bwana," said Viswell, "I will stay and guard the jeep."

"Good idea, Viswell," I responded.

Karen and I got out and made our way through the crowd to a narrow, gated doorway leading into the market. Admission was somewhat exclusive. I saw every Malawian had to either produce or purchase on-the-spot a Malawi Congress Party card for one kwacha, about a quarter, in order to gain entrance - not a trivial expense when per capita income was about two-hundred dollars a year. I was horrified.

"What kind of democracy is this?" I whispered in her ear.

"One party democracy," she said.

"One party blackmail," I retorted.

Luckily, as foreigners, we were forbidden to be Party members. The gatekeeper let us pass through without a card.

Beyond the fencing, it was an orderly market with smoothed cement pads lined with vendors, selling all kinds of items. Vegetables and fruits were plentiful: cabbage, potatoes, carrots, mangos, and papayas in this season. A section was reserved for dried fish, which smelled inedible to a foreigner but were sought after delicacies by the locals.

The people were colorfully dressed. Most of the women wore blouses with the wrap-around skirts called *chitenje*. Pants of any kind were illegal, I repeat, strictly illegal for women to wear publicly in Malawi. It was a part of Kamuzu Banda's absolute control over his people. He thought pants on women were too provocative.

The men were dressed more ratty-tatty. Africa, I learned, was the last destination for the entire world's umpteen-times reused clothes. There was a certain quaintness in seeing Disney shirts, crimson Harvard jerseys, and Chicago Cubs tee-shirts on men who couldn't have had a clue as to these identities.

Pants on men lacked the redeeming quality of the logos and were typically tattered. Shorts were frowned upon because it reminded the Africans of colonial officers, so pretty much all the men, even in the hottest times, wore long pants.

Karen and I wandered over to that part of the market where art works and gifts were sold. It was a small corner of the market which served mostly expatriates and South African tourists.

"Look at those malachite beads," Karen said, pointing at one of the vendor's wares.

"Nice," I said.

"Check them carefully for chips before you buy."

"Will do," I said, selecting a strand and paying about eight dollars for it.

"And there is an original Chilinda painting," she noticed, pointing to a beautiful stretched-out oil work showing a traditional dance in a village. It was very nice and I bought it for about forty dollars.

Chapter 20

"That was a steal," Karen whispered, "Chilinda is the best artist in the country. He usually doesn't let his art sell in the market like this. You got lucky."

I had heard of this painter, that he was arm-twisted into painting Kamuzu Banda's palaces, mostly trimming and doors but also a mural or two. He had a lot of talent and I felt a twang of remorse at such a bargain price for such great talent.

"Oh, look over there," Karen said quietly, "see that man sitting on the ground without arms?"

How could I not help but notice, it was one of the terrible possibilities of polio. We unabashedly stepped over to him.

"Hello sir, and madame," he said. "Nice to see the lady again."

"Good afternoon," Karen said cheerily.

The man then pointed to some small, wooden, painted scenes of the lakeshore with his feet.

"He paints those using a brush between his toes," Karen told me. "Please buy a few."

I agreed and selected three - the folks at home would never believe me.

"One more purchase," I said to Karen, "I'm about out of kwatcha."

"How about a carving?"

"Great idea."

A few paces over was a selection of wooden carvings; lots of animal and bird figures, but my eyes were drawn to one in particular. It was a totem pole, about two feet high, of African men, some caricatures, some costumed, some carrying spears. I had to have it.

"I really like that one," I said to Karen, "they all seem to be climbing for the top and you know I like that."

Before she could respond, I negotiated with the vendor and bought it for about thirty U.S. dollars. A big, satisfied grin spread across my face as I took hold of the carving.

"Very nice," said Karen, "I'm proud of you. Only you're not getting exactly what you think you're getting."

"How so?" I asked.

"Those African figures on your carving are not climbing for the top."

"They're not?"

"Hardly, each one is trying to pull the one above him down."

Freedom

The day of independence came, 6 July 1964, creating another free, black-run African nation, now proudly called Malawi. The name "Malawi" means "flames" in Chichewa and was selected because it harkened back to the ancient kingdom of *Maravi* run by the Chewa ancestors in the sixteenth and seventeenth centuries.

There was jubilation in the streets. Kamuzu gave a five hour speech, recalling his own heroic efforts at setting the people free, punctuating the enormity of the day for the people of his country.

And his country it was. He was now Prime Minister and took several cabinet portfolios. Overnight his picture appeared in virtually every government office and shop in the country.

With sovereignty control over the people tightened. No matter what the behavior at home, the British were now shut out of the decision-making and control. When the legislative Assembly met, virtually all its members had been hand-picked by Kamuzu Banda, duly elected yes, but only those who first passed his scrutiny to get on the ballot.

The legislative meetings themselves, which had been running quite smoothly in the year before independence, took another tone completely. Honest debate dissipated into rubber-stamp affirmations of Kamuzu Banda's wishes. Opposing views quickly became antagonisms, dissensions, heresies.

No wonder that within three months of shedding the colonial yoke there was an open revolt of Cabinet ministers. They disagreed with several policies now taken by Banda. For one, Banda allowed several white, career civil servants to remain on, believing their competence more important to the new nation than instant Africanization. Another had to do with a hospital fee Banda thought necessary, and his view that pay scales needed to be slowly, not immediately increased in the civil service.

The ministers favored radical action towards the white-ruled Southern Rhodesians and an immediate severing of relations with the Portuguese ruling Mozambique next door. Banda was for continued engagement.

Part of the problem was a generation gap. Kamuzu was already in his sixties and virtually all of his ministers were some thirty years his junior. In Africa, respecting elders is of paramount importance, and this is what Banda expected and demanded. He repeatedly referred to the cabinet ministers as "his boys" and this was taken as demeaning and offensive to the hard-working government executors.

Furthermore, in order to obtain their country's independence virtually all the politicians had agreed that one individual, Dr. Hastings Kamuzu Banda, needed to be raised above all others. The savior, or *Ngwazi*, as he became known, was a political necessity to gain the keys to freedom. Unfortunately, once given, absolute power and authority are rarely relinquished and Kamuzu Banda was no exception. The personality cult which led to freedom became the conduit for absolute control.

The trigger event was a pubic disagreement between Banda and a minister over policy towards Mozambique at an international conference in Cairo. Banda raged and when he returned to Malawi made a public speech, warning the people that even ministers could foment conflict through disagreement with his ideas, and this was unacceptable. He reminded the people of the four cornerstones of the Party, now the nation, "Unity, Loyalty, Discipline and Obedience." No one was above these.

He began receiving anonymous letters which pointed fingers at certain ministers saying that they were agitating in their home districts against the Prime Minister. Back and forth the rumors spread, until a group of ministers decided that the Prime Minister had to be replaced.

Banda took the dramatic step of reenacting preventive detention, something the old Federation had used to arrest and hold Banda himself. He established a new security rule requiring any person he deemed worrisome to be restricted to a specified area and requiring them to report to the police regularly. Sensing the unrest, he banned public meetings in the Southern Region before leaving on a fact-finding mission to the north. Nonetheless, things began to unravel. There was unrest in the south and some deaths occurred as a result. Five ministers resigned and fled the country to Tanzania, Zambia and Mozambique. A chief was murdered in Zomba.

In February 1965, one of the ex-ministers, with a band of two-hundred armed supporters crossed into Malawi from Mozambique. The rebels killed a police officer and his family, took off with additional arms from the outpost, and headed for Zomba. Their intent was to kill Prime Minister Banda and establish a new government. When they reached the Shire River they were stopped by a tactical miscalculation - the single river ferry was tied up on the other side of the broad, crocodile infested river.

Soon the news of the rebellion reached Zomba and troops were sent to confront them. The rebels raced back to Mozambique but were followed. Several were captured and hanged, but not the ex-minister, who escaped across the border. It was a sad chapter in the early history of the nation, but it established with certainty that Dr. Hastings Kamuzu Banda would allow no dissension in the nation.

From the time of the cabinet rebellion onward, almost thirty years forward in time, Kamuzu Banda hunkered down and consolidated power, brutally suppressing all opposition, ruling by decree, setting policy without debate, making sure that all attempts by other persons to bring him down were crushed. In 1966 Malawi became a Republic and Kamuzu Banda was sworn in as its President. In 1971 he offered a constitutional amendment proclaiming himself, Dr. Hastings Kamuzu Banda, President for Life of Malawi.

Malawi as an Independent Nation
on the African Continent 1964

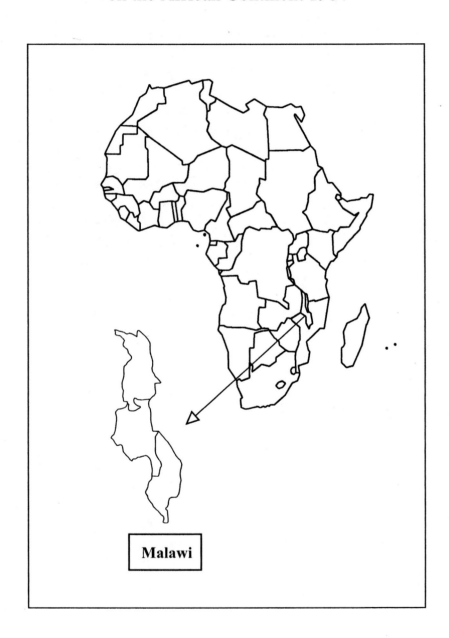

Malawi

Kasungu Adventure

I picked Karen up at her home and we started north to Kasungu National Park on the M1 highway. At first the land was broad and empty but became pock-marked with unnamed granitic peaks further north. I was happy having her next to me, and I kept her appraised of the climbing. This was my last picnic before the bid on the West Face of Chambe Peak.

"You really think that Cite is good enough to climb that face?" she asked.

"I really think that he is damn good," I responded, somewhat testily.

"But I've heard that others, really expert teams, have tried and..."

I finished her sentence, "died."

"Yes," she acknowledged.

"They were drop-in climbers. Didn't know the country. Weren't acclimatized," I argued, trying equally to convince myself and Karen.

Conversation ceased, the miracle of the African landscape enveloping our silence. On this road you roared. There were few people about.

In just a couple of hours we reached the town of Kasungu. Turning west on a paved road, we could see the president's palace at the foot of a mountain.

"The haunted palace?" I asked.

"So thinks H.E.," said Karen, reaching her hand over to mine and covering it softly.

Soon the pavement ended and the road became a thin sand path in the wilderness. I stopped the jeep, got out and locked the wheels into four wheel drive. Acacia, thorn bush, and a hundred other exotic species surrounded the thin track in the bush. A huge pile of elephant manure sat in the middle of the road.

"Don't you love it," Karen said enthusiastically, referring to the spoor.

"Yes," I said, thinking of her and not the dung.

We drove slowly, over fifty kilometers without seeing a soul, the landscape growing wilder and wilder by the minute, until a sign said "Karama Lodge 10k."

The grass was tall and brown. Near a *dambo*, or marshy area, we came upon a huge grey mound, an elephant. I cut the engine and watched the beast feeding on an acacia tree. Its long, wrinkled trunk reached up, plucked a wispy branch and stuffed it down its mouth. After a few minutes it walked away, absolutely silent when it stepped.

We came upon an open area and saw the round wooden-paneled Karama Lodge ahead. I parked the vehicle and we stepped out into the preserve.

Before I knew it, Karen reached over and gave me a big kiss on the lips. It seemed to last a century. Then she said, "I love you."

I took her hand and together we entered the lodge. We registered. A man took our bags from the car to the rondeval, a mud hut with thatched roof and cement floor, that was ours to call home for the weekend.

No sooner had the steward shut the door than we fell into another passionate kiss, deep and sensual and loving. I pulled her body close to mine. We undressed each other like teenagers and rolled onto the bed in a passionate embrace.

There was a half an hour of light left when we went into the lodge dining room for dinner. We sat at a table with a view of the lake. There were no other guests. The waiter brought us two cold Carlsberg beers and took our order for peri-peri chicken.

On the far bank of the lake we saw a herd of kudu, large tanned animals with gracefully twisted antlers, coming down for a drink of water. A flock of Egyptian geese passed over the lodge and skidded to a halt onto the lake, sending a silver shimmering wave outward. At one end of the lakeshore, a pair of crowned cranes stood majestically. It was the Africa that I dreamed of as a boy.

"Most dangerous animal in the bush?" Karen quizzed me.

"Buffalo," I answered.

"No fair, you're right."

"All is fair..." I flirted.

The meal arrived. Peri-peri chicken is a Malawian specialty. The peri-peri is a spicy sauce comparable to tabasco and it was hot, hot, hot. The standard accouterments were provided, french fried potatoes, boiled carrots, and a sprig of parsley. Another two Carlsbergs and the spell was cast. Slowly, imperceptibly, the light disappeared from the world around us. Africa's wild creatures faded from view and I became happily lost in Karen's beautiful expression.

The next morning I woke before sunrise to see Karen peacefully at sleep next to me. I rapped gently on her shoulder. "Get up sleepy," I said, "time for the morning game drive." I ran my fingers through her disheveled black hair, thinking she would jump up at the chance.

"Remember, you're the scout," I whispered in her ear. A smile crossed onto her face but her eyes stayed shut.

"I need a little more sleep, pussy cat," she purred. "You do the morning drive by yourself, then we'll have breakfast together afterwards."

"I'll be back in two hours," I said, covering her up snugly before stepping out of the rondeval into the adventure of Africa.

The faintest orange line brightened the east. The temperature was cool, the air clear as glass. It was ideal for game viewing. I got into the jeep and turned on the motor. The mechanical sound intruded on the solemnity of the morning, but it couldn't be helped. The preserve was large and it was better to get away from the lodge.

I headed for Black Rock, a small out-cropping shown on the map, from which I could survey the land once it got lighter. Driving down the sandy track, I opened the windows and listened to Africa wake up. The raucous call of Green Loeries echoed from the trees and I heard the swish of geese landing on the lake.

Further down the road my headlights illuminated several pairs of red eyes, three hyenas; large, grey, hump-backed beasts standing over a kill. The carcass completely blocked the road. When I drove up next to the corpse, the three predators loped down the road the opposite way, laughing eerily.

I stopped the jeep. The abundant forest kept me from driving around the body. There was no choice but to get out and drag it off the road. Once I cut the engine and stepped outside the jeep, I felt a strange vulnerability. I looked around in every direction but saw nothing unusual.

Stepping over to the dead body, I reached down and felt the tan coat. It was still warm. Blood trickled off its hind legs. A tear across the throat told the story of the last moments of life.

It was a male Reedbuck, a bit smaller than a North American white-tailed deer. It had two short, pointy antlers. I grabbed them and dragged the body off the road, leaving a red smear on the sand. Feeling nervous, I jumped back into the jeep as quickly as I could.

The life of a predator and the death of prey, both part of the natural balance, I reminded myself. With the engine running again, and the heat turned on full, I felt protected. It was not much further until I reached Black Rock.

Silencing the gritty engine, I got out and trotted up to the top of the rock pile just as the blazing sun rose. Scanning the panorama of the landscape, it was refreshing to see no human signs. Or was there one?

I noticed a wisp of smoke, not far away. A bush fire? Possibly. A lightning strike? No rain in days. The fire looked contained. Poachers? Curiosity, not heroism, guided my actions. I ran down the rocky hill, jumped into the jeep and headed in the direction of the smoke. Following a faintly visible track through Brachystegia forest, I came to within a few hundred yards of the still rising smoke, cut the engine and got out.

Poaching was a big problem in the park. There were a lot of elephants and their ivory tusks brought a good price on the black market. The skin of a Nyala, Reedbuck, leopard or lion more than equaled a year's wage. In the name of conservation, I slowly crept towards the suspicious smoke.

I came to a small clearing. No one in sight. At the base of a single tree, a smoky fire stewed. A hole in the tree and a comb of wax on the ground showed the signs of a honey robber.

Then I saw a shadowy figure stepping towards me from behind the tree.

"Hexy," I gasped.

"Yes, boss," said the man who used to work for me, the thief, imposter, the man who took my name for money. He was not at all dressed in his usual suit. He wore animal skins and pointed an ancient blunderbuss at me.

"You have caused me much grief," he said, a mad frown crossing onto his face.

"You're the embezzler," I reminded him.

"That money's not even yours," he answered as though cursing me. "If you'd overlooked it, I wouldn't have had to flee Lilongwe."

"Hexy, it was your choice to steal."

"And now it's my choice to put a bullet through you," he said with deadly seriousness, stepping my way.

The ancient rifle was short and stubby but heavy and powerful enough to kill.

"You'll never get out of this park," I said, "some rangers are not far behind me." I bluffed.

The black smoke surrounded us, but he was close enough, about twenty feet away, that it wouldn't matter. I heard the rusty metal trigger of the gun being cocked, announcing the end of my life.

Just then, out of the black smoke directly behind Hexy, I saw a huge grey form, an elephant with white, blazing tusks silently charging out of nowhere. I only had time to leap sideways

87

to the ground but out of my peripheral vision I saw the elephant run directly into Hexy, knocking him flat out. The gun went off, missing me and falling to the ground inert.

The elephant was as surprised as Hexy or I, but when it realized that a human had gotten in its path, it became enraged, stopped and picked the African up with its trunk like a twig, lifting him high over his great wrinkled head then brutally slammed him to the ground.

I got up and began running towards the jeep, looking back at the very moment one of the tusks pierced Hexy's belly, spraying blood onto the pearly white ivory. An inhuman death cry echoed through the jungle.

I reached the jeep out of breath, climbed in and gunned the engine.

Back at the lodge, I told the story to one of the game scouts and he set out to investigate. I dragged myself over to the rondeval with Karen inside.

When I opened the door, bedraggled and dirt-covered, Karen looked up and exclaimed, "What on earth happened to you?"

"If I tell you, you're going to have to marry me," I said, "and when we go back to the States, no elephants or embezzlers."

She looked surprised, but elated, and came running up to hug me. "I will! When can we get married?"

"After I climb the West Face of Chambe Peak."

The Great Game

Geopolitics was a game Kamuzu Banda played as a realist. True, not long after assuming power in the 1960s he had laid claim to all of Lake Malawi, parts of Tanzania, Mozambique, and Zambia. But rather than duke it out with his neighbors, he backed off and the borders remained as cut in colonial times.

South Africa, bastion of white apartheid rule, was the antichrist of black Africa. Yet it was also the beachhead of Western culture, progress, and wealth. Every other free black African nation publicly spurned South Africa but not Hastings Banda's Malawi.

In 1967, within a year of Malawi becoming a republic, Kamuzu Banda became the first black African leader to establish diplomatic relations with South Africa. He was rewarded with cash, trade, and access which continued until the end of his life.

In 1971, Kamuzu Banda became the first black African leader to visit South Africa, and South Africans, frozen out of the rest of Africa, were accepted in Malawi. To them it became the "Warm Heart of Africa," a frequent tourist destination and investment spot.

In fact, several of the other free African countries also did business with South Africa, but surreptitiously, through third-parties, in unmarked caravans traveling at night, skirting direct borders and coming round the other side. They each sucked the nectar South Africa provided, distasteful as was its politics.

The other African leaders constantly scolded Banda for his open relationship with South Africa. He responded unrepentant, brashly exposing their hypocrisy and calling the relationship a necessary reality which all young African nations should accept.

This is not to say that Kamuzu approved of or accepted apartheid, he bitterly opposed the institutional racism of South Africa. It was a moral outrage, a scourge at the southern tip of the continent that needed to be rectified. His public approach, however, was to engage the whites, show them the culture of

Africa, exchange ideas, and persuade them out of their ignorance and fear.

On the other hand, he secretly supported the struggle of his African brothers and sisters with financing, particularly during the last years of the freedom struggle. Nelson Mandela, the first elected black leader of South Africa, reminisced about Kamuzu after the Malawian leader's death. He said that Kamuzu did a lot of things to help his struggle but quietly, including giving Mandela's party, the African National Congress, a large sum of money as soon as Mandela was released from prison in 1990.

Malawi's relationship with Britain was as a member of the Commonwealth which Banda once said was the "best club in the world." To his misdeeds, the British looked the other way, until the very last years. When Kamuzu traveled to Britain, the Home Office rolled out the red carpet and he was warmly received by the Queen. They were consistent aid providers. He shopped at Harods and took airplanes full of goods back to Malawi.

There were some geopolitical melees that Banda could not avoid. The most significant of these was the civil war in Mozambique. First colonized in the 1500s by seafaring adventurers, the grip of Portugal was deeply imbedded but not strong enough to survive the independence movement.

The civil war in Mozambique broke out in 1975 when the Portuguese abandoned their colony, leaving it free but unstable. This left two African factions. The minority were those loyal to and acculturated by the Portuguese, clandestinely supported by South Africa. And those of the new Republic of Mozambique carrying Marxist sympathies and bankrolled by the Russians and Cubans. It was a struggle fueled by the Cold War that continued for almost twenty years, and not a stone was left untouched, no family unscathed.

For a long while the conflict was contained and the victims internally displaced. In the late 1980s the walls crumbled and a flood of Mozambican refugees poured into Malawi. They fled barbarism on both sides the civil war as whole villages were burned to the ground, babies slaughtered by bayonet and crops destroyed. By 1989, over one million Mozambicans had sought refuge in Malawi.

Perhaps he had no choice, but the aging Banda took the high road with respect to the refugees. He welcomed them as brothers and sisters and allowed aid agencies to feed and clothe the visitors. Camps were established and the influx of more than a million lived in harmony with Malawians until they could return to Mozambique in the mid 1990s at the settlement of the conflict.

However, the struggle had crippling economic consequences for Malawi in the form of the recurrent sabotage of the railway lines which led from Malawi to ocean ports in Mozambique at Ncala and Beira. These railway lines were the most direct link for all goods coming and going.

When rebels were able to, they blew up railroad bridges, bent tracks out of shape or simply carted away whole portions of the line. This recurred to the point where the concourses were completely debilitated. Not until the end of the civil war did these lines of travel open up again and then at great expense.

The alternative was trucking goods overland through Zambia to the west, then south through Zimbabwe into South Africa. This destination was a point of contention with Malawi's African neighbors, though tolerated. The northern alternative was through Tanzania, but the roads were not even fully paved and the port of Dar es Salaam was a sink of corruption, physically incapable of increasing its load to accommodate Malawi's needs.

The result of this crippling loss of efficient transportation routes was a heavy burden of increased cost, undependable supply and export avenues. It never ceased while Hastings Banda ruled through the 1980s and into the 1990s.

Meanwhile, the stewing Cold War, partially being fought in Mozambique, more subtly debated in Nyere's socialist Tanzania, was on the doorstep of Malawi. America viewed Banda as a stalwart of non-communism, not exactly a democrat, but definitely not a communist; and America was willing to pay for this position. In fact, America was one of the first nations to support Malawi at the time of freedom in the 1960s.

So the United States government began increasing its foreign aid to the Republic of Malawi, which is to say, they increased their support of the Life President. And what better way than to export a few computers and a lone trainer to the Ministry of Health.

Call to Dance

Packing the equipment needed to climb the West Face of Chambe Peak involved imagining the unimaginable. How much water would we need? Should I bring a double rack of *climbing hardware*? What kind of food to carry? How many ropes? I was sorting through the gear after lunch when Nelson, the cook, silently entered the room.

"Bwana?"

"Yes Nelson, what can I do for you?" I said, without looking up. In fact, Nelson was always doing for me but I frequently answered him in this way.

"Those people in the village on the far side of Nkhoma Mountain have heard that you and Cite are going to climb that mountain in the south and they want to hold an *ngoma* for you tonight."

"What's an *ngoma*?"

"A traditional dance."

"How could they know that we are going to try that climb?" I asked, surprised that our little undertaking was public knowledge.

"Bush telegraph, sir."

Of course, Nelson did not mean a literal telegraph with wires and posts but a word-of-mouth chain of communications linking village to village, sometimes broadcast by drum, but mostly just person to person.

"Hum," I answered, not sure I wanted to spend my last night out in the bush before the drive south to the climb.

"I don't think so Nelson, I'm too busy."

"Bwana," the cook said in a very under-stated tone, "it would be good for you to have the *ngoma*."

"Why?" I asked. It seemed like an unnecessary expense of time and energy on everyone's part. I was going to need all I had in the next few days.

"That mountain is bad," he said with conviction. "People know this everywhere. The villagers just want to give you some power. I think you will need it."

"Ridiculous, Nelson, all I need is this gear and Cite and we'll be okay."

Just then a clap of thunder echoed outside and the tin roof began rattling with some kind of bombardment.

"What the heck," I said to myself. "Let's see what this is all about Nelson."

"Yes, sir."

We quickly stepped out to the screened-in porch as the noise grew unbearable and saw the most amazing sight. It was hailing. Marble-sized ice pellets rained down upon the house and nearby plains. I saw the guard duck into his small watch post and heard dogs howling as they were stung by the pellets.

In two or three minutes, no more, the hail stopped and the black cloud it emptied from was swept away by a great gust of wind. Just as suddenly, the brightest sunlight flooded the sky. It looked like a hundred years of haze were washed away revealing a land more beautiful than any I had ever known, though it was the same familiar patio view I knew so well.

Around the yard the earth shone a muted pink and glittered like a field of diamonds. I stood speechless. There was absolute stillness, all things had been momentarily silenced by the ice. But the life of ice slips quickly away in Africa. The spell was broken by Nelson's three children who ran out from their quarters and began exploring the strange crystal remains. They ate them, threw them, crushed them, flicked them, spun them with glee. In a span of just ten minutes every single untouched ball of ice melted and the children were left bewildered.

"Nelson," I said, still mystified at the sudden ice storm in Africa. "Let's have that *ngoma*."

The Dance

The metal gate clanked open and Cite and I walked outside to meet the guide who was to lead us to the *ngoma*. A man in his twenties met us, Cite spoke a few words in Chichewa, and we headed out onto one of the myriad paths that meandered through the maize fields on a dark and moonless night.

We walked for almost an hour. My eyes slowly adjusted to night but I still tripped several times, catching myself before tumbling to the ground. We crossed a creek on a log bridge and came to a village with a few fires burning.

There was some discussion with Cite and we were taken to the middle of the circle of huts. Chairs were brought out for us to sit on. The Malawi Congress Party representative greeted me in English, and also the village chief, who spoke no English.

We sat down and a group of children and women assembled nearby. A tall man came out with a large wooden drum and set up to one side. The nearest fire was stoked.

Out of the darkness came a figure in costume. He wore a sleeveless shirt made of *chitenje* material with the Life President's face on his back and chest. His naked arms bore epaulets made of black straps and feathers. A leather loin-cloth covered his private parts. His face was painted in red, green and black and more feathers stood on top of his head, held by a band, making him look abnormally tall. He wore bells on his ankles and was barefoot.

The drumming began with an intermittent rhythm. The man in costume began dancing slowly, more like walking in place. The bells on his ankles immediately sounded the dancer's motion. I smelled wood smoke and saw other people in dim light at the periphery. Gradually, the dancer sped up, leading the drum beat. For a meek looking man, he gained strength and vitality the faster he moved, raising his legs higher and higher into the air. The chiming bells grew louder and faster. Then one of the ankle bells fell off and everyone stopped.

The dancer bent over calmly and refastened the bells around his slim ankle. He began dancing again at the same slow pace he initiated at the start. The drummer picked up exactly as before, joined by a chorus of women and children chanting synchronously with the dance. The pace built up again to a frenzy; bells chiming, drums beating, human voices crying out in the moonless night. Just as the dancer seemed to jump into the black sky, the bells on his other ankle fell off and he stopped to replace them.

My American perspective first thought this was a sign of incompetence. Why not lock those suckers on? I thought. Then I realized that the unexpected falling off of the bells was part of the dance, not a disappointment, intrusion or mistake.

The ritual started all over again, but now I saw sweat dripping down the man, staining the face of Kamuzu Banda on his shirt. The dancer's muscles swelled and his leanness filled out to that of a perfect human form. I was drawn into the dance, watching details through a magnifying glass. I saw individual feathers bending and swirling; grains of sand kicked up and drifting back to the earth; and smoke bent and thrown by the dancer's motion.

Again and again, for hours, the dancer, drummer, women and children, kept up the *ngoma* in a superhuman effort of endurance. I was hypnotized, I can think of no other comparison, and when the fires died down and chill crept up on me, it was a gentle rapping on my shoulder by Cite that snapped me out of the *ngoma* dream world. No words were said when it ended. The dancer just removed the bells and stepped away into the darkness. The drummer disappeared and the villagers melted away into their huts. I followed Cite back through the fields until the hollow metal bang of my gate closed behind me.

No one had explained the dance. I didn't know what it meant, but I accepted it in all its utter difference. For all my skepticism, I now felt internally prepared by African kin to challenge the greatest rock face in all the continent.

Absolute Power

Brutality was the sting of his lion-tail fly whisk rising angrily behind palace walls, lashing out far into the countryside. Banda's opponents knew his scourge as a life sentence in a dank cell at Mikuyu Prison in Zomba without attorney, trial or jury; tortured by cane beatings, held in leg-irons or straightjackets. In villages, his wrath meant a brother's nighttime beating at the hands of the paramilitary Young Pioneers leaving a bleeding, broken, submissive cripple and trembling extended family. To the disloyal ministers, his ire played out as a faked car accident with the already dead bodies stuffed into a blue Peugeot and rolled over a cliff.

An expatriate inside Malawi could only see that which was presented to him, but shadowy truths leaked out in rumors, whispered stories and outside news. Apologists for his brutality are doing a job no one asked to be done, not even *Kamuzu* himself, who once said that his opponents would become "food for crocodiles."

Absolute control meant only one political party, only one newspaper, one radio station, no television, no public debate and a self-declared President for Life in 1971. Just as a master is a slave to the demands of total control, *Kamuzu* Banda became paranoid and truth slipped away from his reign as the years passed.

The annual crop inspection was a glaring example of this. Matching the surreal scene with the black helicopter, the French pilot, and the cheering crowds in the stadium of ten thousand, were his annual crop inspections during the late 1980s. Banda told the world and his people that Malawi was self-sufficient in food but the truth was far from that. His sycophants assured that he saw exactly what he imagined.

When Kamuzu Banda rose out of the stadium and flew out to the countryside on crop inspection, he was taken to specially prepared fields, seeded with hybrid corn, richly fertilized, doused with pesticides, tended by professionals, and purged of raiding

97

baboons with rifle and bullet. When he touched down, it was over the rainbow, to a field bursting with corn grown taller than an elephant's eye. The truth at the time was extreme poverty and a painful cycle of hunger that his people endured year after year.

Stop after stop confirmed the bounty of the agrarian world Hastings Banda created for his people in his mind. Along the way he visited the tobacco plantations, the chief export of the country, of which he was a primary owner. To keep the sotweed flowing, villagers were pressured to grow the inedible commodity in lieu of subsistence foods dearly needed.

At the end of the day, when the helicopter returned to the palace stadium, all the people would be waiting there for him to hear the results of the journey. They did not volunteer but were required to be there.

The big Party men stood their ground near exits and on the dusty field. Sweating profusely, sunlight glinting off the small, round buttons with the Life President's face pinned to their lapels, their job was assuring absolute obedience from the people.

And there could be only one rejoinder from the Life President upon his return from the fields, how the bounty of Malawi was once again free flowing, that there was plenty in the land, and that they owed it all to Kamuzu.

Chapter 26

A Climber's View of Malawi 1988

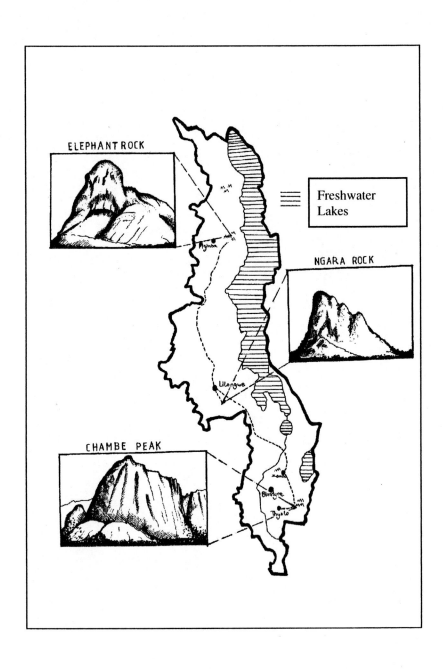

Chambe Peak

Roaring south on a ribbon of black tarmac, in a creamy white jeep, my Malawian climbing partner, Cite, sat silently next to me, stoically lining up to be the first Malawian to challenge the great West Face of Chambe Peak, a more than vertical mile of unclimbed rock. Not speaking the same language, his entire briefing was translated by the cook, in the shade of a jacaranda tree.

The climbs Cite and I made during our training for Chambe Peak are recorded in Malawian history - Elephant Rock in the north, Ngara in the Central Region, and the slabs on the East Face of Chambe Peak. Together we learned how to climb in Africa like no multi-racial team had ever climbed, and we always kept the prize in mind. Now it was time to try for the ultimate ascent - the West Face of Chambe.

Ten days were allotted for the tour. One just to drive get down to Mulanje in the south. A second day to assemble a team of porters and build a base camp. Up to six days to climb the face itself and get back down. A day of rest and one to drive home. Cite, the man, was a character I had to consider.

He was a man of integrity, humble and hard working with a spirit that did not give up. Cite had his own thirst for adventure and he climbed for himself and his country. Nobility is a simple man with a big heart. My African partner was such a man.

At Likabula Forestry station, we gathered a team of porters to carry our gear to a base camp at the foot of the mountain. The head porter, a man named Dawson, was wiry thin with an ant-like head and scrawny arms. He spoke English and knew the mountain as well as any man alive. I had worked with him on several trips onto the massif and knew he was brave, honest, and trustworthy.

The next morning he brought six other porters. It was difficult even to recruit these men. He said it was bad luck to go up to that face. There were many stories about Mulanje, and superstitions were rampant and believed. One of the most curious stories was about little green men.

According to Dawson, these little green men lived on the top of the massif and possibly on the West Face of Chambe Peak itself. Legend tells that when a person is walking alone on Mulanje, he or she can come across a fully prepared meal out in the middle of nowhere. Those who partake in the meal are destined to become forever lost on the mountain. Dawson himself came across such a feast once, but he fled and survived.

I watched Cite as the story was told; he asked questions and was answered in his native Chichewa. I worried that it might scare him and that our attempt might not even get off the ground. I was wrong in my hesitation, for Cite said, in his halting English, after all the stories were told, "We will climb that mountain."

From Likabula Forestry Station we set out on foot, nine of us in a line, walking in old fashion safari style through the African bush towards the bottom of the West Face. I saw the massive profile ahead of us, a two-tier behemoth of reddish-blue rock and I gasped. No nightmare could ever present a more imposing wall of rock. I felt a momentary weakness but did not let it show.

In two hours time we reached that spot at the base of the lower wall where a weakness broke through the otherwise smooth face.

"Set up camp," I ordered Dawson, "Cite and I will climb up a couple of rope lengths and return for the night."

"Yes bwana," he responded, not questioning my methods.

"Cite," I called to my partner, "ready?"

"Ready."

We put on the now familiar gear; climbing harnesses, rock shoes, a rack of climbing hardware worthy of a Yosemite team. Cite uncoiled one of our two ropes. He anchored himself to a tree and put the rope through a *belay device*, which created enough friction so that if I fell, he could hold me.

"Climbing," I called, about to become a living part of the giant face.

"Climb," he said, in a business-like manner.

Before stepping onto the rock, I cast one last smile at him, a deep, hopeful smile, but I could not promise.

I stepped onto the wall, caressed the rock like a lover and suddenly felt elated. We were at the crossroads. It was ours to take. This was audacious.

I focused on the next few moves, which were not difficult. The friction between my rubber shoes and the rock was good, very good.

Silently, I connected step after step with the rock, moving swiftly, until I came to a vellozia bush growing out of a pad of earth stuck to the wall about thirty feet up. It felt relatively solid. I girthed it with a piece of sling webbing, clipped a *carabiner* to it and fed the rope through the gate. Now, if I fell, it would be up to Cite to hold me.

In another fifty feet I reached the mouth of the chimney that I knew cut almost all the way to the top of the lower slab, nearly 2,000 feet higher. I found a small crack, put in a six-sided aluminum nut, and clipped the rope into its attached sling. Another piece of protection, a temporary reprieve from the risk of a long fall. I was on my way.

Fear, enemy of the climber, dissipated and I began to stride up the chimney, spreading my arms and legs between the four foot gap, climbing vertically with the rope dangling away between my legs. I clipped a few more sturdy vellozia branches - this was Africa and the climbs were organic - and I was soon at the end of the rope, 150 feet up.

I set a solid three-point anchor, put the rope through my own belay device, and called down for Cite to climb. In a moment he started up. I watched him make the first few moves with confidence and then my vision drifted off to the wall around me. We weren't very high up the face but all around me was the sea of rock, the lower wall of the West Face of Chambe Peak.

Cite climbed well and fast. When he reached me, he wore a big smile, a bold smile, a possible hero's smile. It would not be this easy, I knew, but morale was everything. I was pleased.

He clipped himself into the anchor. I took the lead again, that was my role, the sharp end of the rope. The chimney simply continued up, up, up and away. Striding up the steep wall, I looked down at the base and saw the porters setting up the tents. They were already looking small, stick figures bound to flatland.

Making my way up another 150 feet, I established a second anchor station. I tied-off the rope and rappelled, that is I slid down the anchored rope, until I reached Cite. That was it for the day, 300 feet of progress. We could go up no further without committing ourselves to the face. Both ropes were left in place. Next morning we would use ascending devices to climb up the two ropes and continue from the high point.

Cite rappelled to the ground and I followed. Hell of a start, I thought, a good day and a good omen. Afternoon was passing. I was exhausted. The porters built a fire and began cooking a huge feast. It would be our last for at least another three days.

After the tension of starting the climb faded and we were all sitting around camp relaxing, I became invisible. The Africans conversed in Chichewa, the camp was active and happy. I had my own little African village and a mark of thin, colorful ribbon, our ropes, decorated the face of Chambe as never before.

The next morning Cite and I piled down a breakfast like it was our last. The two packs were loaded, mostly with water and high energy foods like nuts and jerky. We brought hard candy to suck on, aimed at reducing the inevitable feeling of thirst.

The first act was to ascend the fixed ropes, a technique we had practiced. Cite departed first and there was a touching farewell between him and his African brothers. They exchanged words in a language I did not know, but in human and universal tones I felt.

When we reached the top of the second rope, it was my turn to lead again. Cite tied into the anchor, I organized the rack of protective gear on a sling around my shoulder and took off.

The great chimney now took me inside it, a comforting way to climb, and I made rapid progress. I reached the end of the rope and Cite followed speedily. On a mountain of this size, speed is essential and Cite's pace matched mine yard for yard.

At one point the great yawn of the chimney was so deep that Cite suggested that we climb unroped, simultaneously, to increase speed. It was risky, if one of us fell it could be fatal to both, but the combination of sturdy vellozias, a perfectly sized chimney and the need for speed convinced me to go for it. We each dragged a rope and climbed within a few feet of each other - free soloing on the biggest wall in Africa. He was right. We made rapid progress.

Suddenly, the chimney topped out and the slab of rock eased back. We found ourselves on a low-angled portion of the lower slab but saw a short, fierce headwall above. We'd have to surmount that in order to complete the lower 2,000 feet.

Trotting up the slab, the chime of metal clanking in the great hall of nature, we were still strong, bold, unsubmissive. We reached the headwall and it looked hard.

I picked a spot where a watermark showed that in the rainy season the waters poured down. The rock was white, smooth and appealing. We set a belay anchor and I began the lead. This was Yosemite quality rock and I had been a Yosemite climber. A few rare cracks presented themselves and I was able to put in adequate protection as I climbed upward.

Leading the rope length took over an hour to complete. Tense climbing, of unknown difficulty but as hard as any Cite and I had found in our Malawi adventures. When I topped out, I saw the ledge separating the two rocky sections of Chambe, a hanging garden of several hundred yards which ended where the upper 3,500 feet of wall reared up. I turned away and concentrated on giving Cite a tight belay.

At one point in his climbing, I felt a slip, the rope tightened in the belay device and my harness drew tight around my waist but it held. Without an exchange of words, a brief second of insecurity passing, I felt the rope go slack again as Cite found his purchase and continued climbing. When he reached me, neither of us made a comment.

The base of the upper section of cliff looked close but it was deceptive. The vegetation was thick and thorn-ridden. Having already climbed 2,000 feet, we were tired. Fighting the thick bush drained us further and what we thought would be a short, happy amble became a desperate struggle.

Upon reaching the upper wall, streaked in dirt and blood from the cat-claws, I fell to the ground exhausted, panting and completely spent. That was the easy part of the climb, the first 2,000 feet and the scramble on the ledge. The real endurance test was above us.

I looked up and saw an unending expanse of rock soaring to the heavens. It was solid, massive, without feeling or weakness. From the ledge we could decide to back off, to scramble down from the ledge at one side and then limp back to Likabula. It was a decision I had to make, but I would give us a night's rest and see if the same feeling of dread awaited me in the morning.

Turning Point

In the last years of Hastings Banda's reign his vitriol drifted to subordinates and the elements of state he created and released. His right-hand man and his niece, the "official hostess," worked Kamuzu like a puppet on strings. Partially it was the leader's advanced age, at least in the upper eighties but possibly in his nineties, partially it was the nearly twenty years of solitude that being the Life President had brought him.

Among the state apparatus that kept the people under control was the single newspaper that spoke only the political will of Banda. The competition was banned. The sole political party, the Malawi Congress Party, had an assigned representative in each village, no matter how small or how remote. They were the omniscient eyes and the ears of the state. If you or a family member crossed that person, personally or politically, swift reprisal followed. The neo-nazi Young Pioneers indoctrinated youth, although most of the 'young' Pioneers were older adolescents and people in their twenties or thirties - they were not boy scouts.

Meanwhile, Kamuzu himself slipped into a dream-like senility. He no longer trusted western medicine, at least not in Malawi, where he trusted only a witch doctor somewhere in the hills of Zomba District. If he got really sick, he went to South Africa where apartheid medicine offered the latest pharmaceutical and advanced surgery.

There were no less than six palaces in the country. In his home area of Kasungu, he refused to use the palace believing it haunted. By whom, by what spirit, we never found out, but he did not stay there in his later years because of this ghost.

In the capital, Lilongwe, he stayed at Mtunthama Palace while his new palace on the other side of town was being built at an estimated cost of one hundred million dollars. Inside the new palace were three elevators, about half the number in the entire country. The interior fixtures were gathered from around the world by the official hostess and carefully installed by the best craftsmen available.

Banda's communications with the people were in English only, by now he had forgotten his own language. The party ran the radio station and the only talk radio, for the few who had telephones to call in, were health shows.

Behind dark glasses, wearing fine European suits, covering his head with a black homburg, he was seen less and less by the people. The annual crop inspections were the most visible exceptions to his reclusiveness. More and more it was the small cadre of people that spoke and acted for Kamuzu.

The country, on the other hand, isolated as Kamuzu Banda wanted it to be, was not immune to world events. As the Cold War struggle defined the 1980s, Banda received more and more foreign aid with strings attached.

Regional and global economies left Malawi behind, only rearing its ugly international head in recession, currency devaluations, price inflations, and dependence on outside fertilizers to make the weary land grow subsistence crops. Foreign exchange currency earned through tobacco, tea and a small, lovely crop of macadamia nuts created more dependence and less subsistence across the country.

Just as in the autumn of any dictatorial patriarch, the leaves of his people's despair came floating down around him: poverty, hunger, illiteracy, over population, an epidemic of AIDS. The remaining question was whether Dr. Hastings Kamuzu Banda was completely blind to this people's suffering and determined to take his people with him on a final path of utter destruction.

Shadows on the Wall

Morning twilight was pink and orange and indescribably beautiful. I slept deeply and felt much better than at the end of the previous day. Cite was chipper, singing to himself as he built a fire, looking no worse for the wear. He gave no sign of wanting to retreat.

Before I saw the rising sun itself, the shadow of Chambe appeared, an unmistakable widow's peak of darkness, extending outward forty or fifty miles into the plains.

Then, before my very eyes, the shadow came racing back towards us as the sun continued its daily rise. It made me feel as if a speeding locomotive was barreling towards me, and when the titanic shadow collided with the mountain, I literally felt its crash as a warm breeze covering my body. Climb on, I decided for myself, press on.

We saddled up, gear reattached, ropes paid out and I started up the steep beginning of the 3,500 feet leading to the top. It was hard climbing with poor protection. I grunted a few times. The moves were desperate.

I was going for another chimney about eighty feet up, but the slab was steep and clean. One slip and I was going for a grounder. I backed off, climbing back down the few feet I attained, and left the pack. I could haul it up after reaching the next belay spot.

Without the weight and encumbrance of the pack, the odds shifted my way. I was light as a shadow and strong. Move by move, I followed an invisible ladder of nubbins and edges, until I reached the chimney and a sturdy vellozia for a belay anchor. Cite tied my pack onto the rope and I hauled it up and then I hauled his pack up.

I worried that this was harder than anything I'd put him up against so far. But as he had done so many times before, Cite surprised me. He virtually ran up the wall, and was at my side before I knew it.

The chimney shot up, dead vertical, for rope length after rope length, until I counted a thousand feet put under us. This was for the gold. There were fewer anchor points, meaning higher risk should a lead fall occur but now I was rising to my own best.

We were far above the ledge now, even rising above neighboring peaks along the edge of the massif but it just kept coming. Things were going well, until I came to a point where the chimney was blocked by a blank, twenty-foot overhang beset by unclimbable alternatives.

"Damn it," I said. "Impossible," I thought. I did not have a bolt kit with me which I could used to aid our way over the obstacle. We were locked out, fully committed to the wall, beyond the point of return. We were checkmated. A moment of crippling fear overcame me. I hung on the anchored rope, silently defeated, as Cite climbed up to me on belay.

When he reached me, Cite immediately realized the gravity of the situation but reacted differently. People had said to me that he was "juju," some kind of sorcerer, but I had scoffed at their superstition. If he had any magic, we needed it now.

I was despondent, frozen, helpless. I clung onto the rock as if it were a mother's breast. I watched Cite pull up the second rope. He eyed the wall and the restart of the chimney only a few body lengths above us. There was no hope of going either up or down, I thought. There was no hope at all.

The small African man, who had been a stout follower throughout virtually all of our adventures, took up a few coils of the second rope near its free end and hung his body out into space, pulling tightly at the anchors. His black arm swirled in the empty space, faster and faster until he let the coils loose, sending them up the impossible wall towards the chimney.

What is he doing? I asked to myself. The rope came tumbling down empty, a bit of rock and gravel skidding noisily into space. Undaunted he gathered up the coils again, strained outward even further into the void and swung his arm circularly with great precision and purpose. He sent the coils upward as he fell hard against the rock wall.

I caught him and made sure he went no further than a few feet but he hit his head against the rock. A trail of blood splattered across the back of his head.

My attention was locked on Cite.

"Cite!" I shouted, "are you okay?"

He shook his head, he was conscious, and managed an "okay."

"The rope, the rope, what happened to the rope," I thought out loud. I looked up the death wall and there I saw the rope hanging down, two strands, motionless, across the full length of the overhang. The middle was, apparently caught on something in the chimney above.

"Bush," said Cite, climbing back to the small perch we shared. I stepped out to the lip where he was stationed and craned my neck until I saw a small vellozia just back from the edge of the chimney, invisible from where I had been cowering. That son-of-a-gun, he's lassoed the bush, he is juju!

I pulled him over to the inside of the chimney and motioned for him to put me on belay. Then I secured the free end, and the middle section of the rope hanging above us - fixing the line.

I took out a pair of the ascending devices and attached them to one strand of rope. Gently, ever so gently, I pulled on the rope. The real test was body weight and I gradually stepped into a stirrup attached to the *ascender*.

"My turn," I said, as Cite looked groggily up at me.

Inch after inch, I alternately slid one after the other ascender up the rope while putting my weight on the one locked into place. Inches grew to feet, trickles of dirt told me that the bush was not going to last forever, and I cautiously steamed up the rope.

At last I reached the lip of the chimney and saw the puny vellozia bush that held and gave me life on this inhuman rock. I pulled over onto the chimney floor like the lowest form of life and then thanked every power I knew of profusely.

A safer anchor was available deeper inside the chimney and Cite soon followed, with me pulling top-rope and him using the ascenders. When I saw that black man's face come over the lip of infinity, I knew we shared a profound brotherly love and tears poured from my eyes, tears of joy even though my body had not a drop of water left to spare.

We bivouacked on the ledge immediately above the nearly fatal overhang. As darkness came upon us, we saw the fires of villagers out on the broad plain nearly a vertical mile below us. First a few flames flickered, then a dozen little lights until the entire view filled with hundreds of evenly spaced fires. Land of fire, Malawi had been called, and now I knew why.

There was enough dead vegetative matter on the ledge for us to light a small fire of our own. How many stories our little light kindled that night I'll never know. But even without the flame, a legend was born, and I was thankful.

Our water supply was running low. My lips had cracked and split from days of dryness. I found a small succulent growing on the ledge. Its thick leaves proved too tempting and I plucked one. Peeling off the waxy skin, I found the inner substance of its life and spread the cool, thick jell onto my lips, relieving the rawness.

Cite and I slept back to back as the night grew cold. Next morning we saw the same extraordinary display of light and shadow as the day before, but we were noticeably higher and above all the surrounding peaks. It was the day to climb off the beast known as the West Face of Chambe Peak.

The chimney system continued without interruption. It even started to lean slightly off vertical but at this stage of the climb, every move appeared through a haze of fatigue. Dream-like, I fell into a state of utter exhaustion where my every movement played out in slow motion.

Gradually, the climbing became easier and then, after some thirty rope lengths since the start of the upper wall, I saw what I knew was the summit of Chambe.

When the wall finally gave in to easy scrambling, we cast off the rope and continued climbing side by side, dragging ourselves up the last little ridge to the summit of Chambe Peak. On top we shook hands and looked down at the enormity of the climb and our achievement.   The road and the huts below reminded me of miniatures in a child's toy train set, too small to have been where we came from.

The Right Turn

Yellow acacia blossoms covered the car top like melted candle wax. Viswell was ready to drive me to the office for the day's computer training and I climbed into the car. I was recovering from the big climb, feeling well, satisfied and happy. I sat in the back seat and cracked open a two month old copy of a news magazine. The guard opened the black iron gate and we drove off as usual.

It wasn't until I felt the car turn right, off the main road, that I saw our direction was wrong. I became curious.

"Viswell, did I forget an errand for this morning?" There occasioned legitimate tasks which I did not schedule but either Viswell, or Nelson had organized.

"No bwana," he said tersely, stepping on the gas.

I let the silence fall, a hard bwana-like silence which meant I wanted further explanation. I put down the old news and stared forward into the rear-view mirror to catch my driver's eyes.

"Viswell, is there a problem I need to know about?"

"No bwana," he said, ignoring my green glaring eyes in the mirror.

He turned down Mtunthama Way. I had not been to this side of town since going to His Excellency's crop inspection send-off long ago. This was strange and getting stranger.

"Viswell," I said sternly now, regretting that I had let this antic get so far along, "I think we are going the wrong way." Sarcasm was often lost on Viswell, and this proved no exception.

"Bwana, you will see," he answered in a low, passive voice.

"I will see?" I responded angrily, but before I could think of an appropriate command we were next to the stadium outside the palace. No one was there. Viswell slowed down. Good grief, I thought, Viswell has gone bananas.

We approached the palace gates. There was a high brick wall on either side of the gold-painted gates with liana vines growing thick and sprites of orange flowers dangling like fruit. He drove right up to the front gate.

I wanted to shout. I wanted to scream. I wanted to kill Viswell before The Life President's goons killed me, but it was too late. A man wearing a deep blue commando suit and black beret stepped out from a guard booth, toting a machine gun. This was not going to be a nice end for a good man in Africa.

To my surprise, the guard looked carefully at Viswell and signaled someone behind the gate to swing it open. I could not speak. I dared not speak. Viswell drove into the palace grounds.

There was a round stucco building, nearly as big as the stadium a few hundred yards away. A low flight of white marble steps led up to an enormous set of carved wooden doors. Viswell pulled up to the steps and stopped.

"Bwana," he said in an annoyingly calm voice, "you have been invited to have breakfast with Kamuzu."

I was flabbergasted. I suspected all along that Viswell was a spy, but I never thought he might be a good spy. He stepped out of the car and opened my door.

"Bwana," he said with a big smile, the kind of natural, real, hopeful smile which an African can give, "good luck."

At this point I really had no choice. I strode up the Italian marble steps and approached the great wooden doors. The carvings were intricate. Before I could stop to decipher the woodwork, both doors swung outward and two stewards in white uniforms wearing gold fez stepped to the side and stood bolt upright and silent.

A third man, someone I recognized as one of the Life President's closest advisors stepped forward.

"You are welcomed to Mtunthama Palace." He said. "Please come in."

I did as I was told.

"Please follow me," he said turning and leading me down a large, cavernous hallway. It was lit with the most elegant sconces, obviously European, with dull yellow light emanating downward. Our footsteps echoed in the hallway, off glistening pink marble flooring and white walls.

It seemed an interminable walk, and my legs, the legs of a climber, almost buckled but I knew that would be rather embarrassing and I pulled myself together. Keep walking. We passed some rooms. A large, square library where I glimpsed hardwood shelving, slews of fine books, dark brown carpeting. A room painted green, red and black - the national colors. We passed some closed doors. Finally, I could see a room ahead with natural light coming out into the hallway.

The vizier stopped and turned towards me. "His Excellency has asked to meet you. He is pleased about your climb of Chambe Peak, particularly that you brought a Malawian with you. You will be dining with him."

Only a few paces from the room ahead, he added, "He is waiting now."

He motioned me into the room. I stutter stepped under the lintel and emerged in a huge salon with a long, formal table in the center. One side of the room was all glass windows looking out into a luxuriant garden.

Panels decorating the other long wall showed a brief history of Kamuzu's life: birth under the sprawling kachere tree, education at the Scottish mission, the long walk to South Africa, Banda as healer, his return to Nyasaland and on a London stage taking the reigns of power from the colonizers. They were compelling scenes painted with great skill.

Immediately my attention was drawn to the Life President of Malawi, Dr. Hastings Kamuzu Banda, slowly rising from a purple velvet-covered Louis the XIV chair at the far end of the table. I was shaking with fear. I stopped dead in my tracks.

A firm, deep voice said, "Please come in and shake my hand."

"Your Excellency," I squeaked out, "I am most honored by this visit." I stepped forward, walked to the right side of the long table and approached the Big Man of Malawi. I heard the door to the room close behind me.

I felt embarrassed because I towered almost a foot above him. He had such a small frame, round face and wide, flared nose with only a bit of salt and pepper hair dotting his mostly bald head. His ears stuck out from the sides of his head. He wore a three-piece European suit, white shirt and tie with a white handkerchief in his breast pocket. He was a dapper octogenarian.

As I approached him, I held out my right hand, brought my left hand to my right elbow and knelt in a traditional Malawian greeting of respect, casting my eyes downward. He grasped my hand. His was warm, thin and bony, but he squeezed mine tightly and did not let go.

"I wanted to shake the hand of the man who brought a Malawian, the first Malawian, up the greatest rock face in all of Africa," he said. "Jomo has Mt. Kenya, Julious has Kilimanjaro but I have Chambe Peak and it is a bigger climb than either of them."

"Thank you, your Excellency," I managed to say. President Banda was still holding my hand but I had long since learned that African men do hold the hands of other men. It was a sign of friendship.

"Let us eat," he said, finally releasing his grip. "Please sit down."

Kamuzu sat back into the pillowed cushion of his Louis XIV chair at the head of the table and I sat next to him on a more modest blue velvet version of the same chair. He lifted and rang a silver bell.

A steward came out wearing the identical white uniform and fez as the men who opened the palace doors. He carried a silver platter with a half circle top, stopped aside Kamuzu and served. He laid out a small dish of fresh-cut mango in front of him and stepped around to my side of the table and put one before me.

Then a second steward came into the room with two silver carafes. Kamuzu had tea poured into his china cup. I was given coffee.

"We know what you like to eat for breakfast," said the leader of the small African nation with a smile he could not restrain.

"There will be fried potatoes and fresh bacon coming after the mango."

Now I was sure Nelson was a spy too. Oh well, I thought, drink the coffee.

"Was it a difficult climb? I heard it took you four days."

"Your Excellency, it was the hardest climb I have ever done."

"That is good. How was the boy?"

I knew he meant my Malawian partner, Cite, and surely the sixty years or more that separated these two men's ages justified the term 'boy.'

"Your Excellency," I saw no other way to address Dr. Banda, the usual expatriate slang "H.E." would not do, "I would have lost my life a dozen times were it not for Cite. He truly is a hero."

"That he is," said Kamuzu with a beaming smile on his face. The dark, blood-shot eyes lit up, and he welled a small tear of pride as if it had been his own child who accomplished the feat. I looked down at my bowl and started into the mango, which was delicious as an African morning.

"You know I lived in America, once, long ago," he said. "I know how clever you Americans are and how brave."

"Thank you, Your Excellency."

"You could have taken an American. That would have been easier for you. It was very brave to bring one of us," said Dr. Banda.

"I thought it was important. Besides, Cite and I climbed together for months before trying the West Face of Chambe Peak. I knew he could do it," I said. "Even before I came to Malawi, I

119

dreamed I would climb a great face with an African. I've never told that to anyone before," I added, and it was true.

"I admire braveness," he said. "And I have a secret for you."

The mango was finished. I sipped coffee. A steward brought and served the fried potatoes and bacon. Kamuzu had toast and jam. When the steward left the room out a side door *Ngwazi* continued.

"I am the Life President of Malawi, but I have also been a medical doctor in England. Yes, I have treated the terminally ill, white and black, rich and poor, and I know when a tonic is needed."

What was he going to reveal? Would it be one of those 'If I tell you, I'll have to kill you' type of secrets. I really didn't want to know, but I was spellbound and silent.

"Your braveness has been a lesson to me and I am going to act. I am The Life President of Malawi, I am Kamuzu - the first medical doctor from Malawi - the first and only leader of the Malawian people - and this is what I will do for my children."

Please, please, I thought to myself, do not tell me.

He continued, voice growing firmer, one hand squeezing into a fist. "There will be free and democratic elections in Malawi."

I thought, this is impossible. But Dr. Banda continued. "I will allow other political parties to form, I will set a date for elections. The people will vote."

This was shocking news.

"And I will not fix the outcome and if the people decide to throw their Kamuzu out of office," he now spoke in the third person, "he will leave in peace."

Bombshell, this was a political, human bombshell.

"Can you keep my secret?" he asked.

"Your Excellency, as I have put my life on the line to climb Chambe Peak with a Malawian, I will promise not to tell this secret until it is history."

"History it will be," he said with certainty.

My plate was clean, the meal was nearly down to my socks. Kamuzu's toast was also finished.

"You mustn't be too late for work," he said casually, "we want to learn computers too."

Kamuzu Banda rang the silver bell. The door to the room opened and his advisor ushered me out. We walked down the long hall in silence. I never looked back. I stepped outside the great wooden palace doors, swept down the white marble steps and into the waiting car. I never looked back. I never doubted.

Postscript

In 1994 Malawi held free and democratic elections. Dr. Hastings Kamuzu Banda was voted out of office. After departure from office, he was tried and convicted of the murders of several politicians but ultimately acquitted. He then lived quietly in Blantyre until his death in 1997 in a South African hospital.

Disclaimer

This is a historical novel, not a history textbook. The life of Dr. Hastings Kamuzu Banda has been followed fairly carefully, although some authorial license has been taken to simplify the story and add dramatic effect. Banda himself preferred certain versions of his life to those uncovered by historians and reported elsewhere.

The political history of Malawi is considerably more complex than the story reveals. The predecessor party to the Malawi Congress Party, the Nyasaland African Congress, is completely overlooked for simplicity. Many important Malawians have not been named or their stories discussed in order to keep the tale tight.

Admission

The climbing part of the novel is quite autobiographical. I lived in Malawi 1986-1989. Following the adage 'Write about what you know best,' I have woven this fictional tale around real persons and events.

I did train a Malawian, Site Taulo, to climb and together we climbed many (but not all!) of the mountains in Malawi. Site began as a construction worker, and also gardener. Site is a person I hold in the highest esteem and he and I did climb the daunting West Face of Chambe Peak as a team. Officially we were the second party, but Site was the first Malawian. He broke a spell. There was press coverage two weekends in a row. A radio show host posed a future game show question, "Who was the first Malawian to scale the West face of Chambe Peak." Site Taulo was that man.

Acknowledgments

Ten years of thought came crashing down on paper in a brief flurry of writing that became *Breakfast with Kamuzu*. Those family members who helped me during this intense period include: Lisa and Tom Barnes, Mary and Hu Allen, George Allen, Nyika and Jos Allen. Muller Davis Jr. was a valuable reader and editor. Joeff Davis drafted a cover and did me a great favor in moving me along. Good friends whose support I acknowledge include: Gordon and Delia Smith, Vickie Camerlingo, Ben Benjamin and Ed Sklar. Thanks to other readers including Sandy Ashworth and Betsy Granek. Special thanks to Mr. Llolsten Kaonga who helpfully reviewed parts of the manuscript. Thanks to Ruthie Francis for input on the cover text. Deborah Helitzer deserves a thanks for sharing adventures in that far place.

Glossary

African Terms

Assimilato: A Portuguese-Mozambican term referring to a social class of Africans brought into colonial society.

Bwana: An African term meaning boss.

Chambo: A fresh water tilapia fish found in Lake Malawi. Very good to eat.

Chewa: One of the tribes living in Malawi.

Chichewa: One of the local languages of Malawi.

Chimanga: A Chewa word meaning maize or corn.

Chitenje: A wrap-around skirt used in Malawi.

Dambo: A marshy area.

Edzi: A Malawi term for AIDS.

Fodya: A Chewa word meaning tobacco.

Kamuzu: The given forename of Banda, literally meaning "little root" in Chichewa.

Kwacha: Currency unit in Malawi, on the order of a dollar.

Maize: Another term for what Americans call corn.

Mbumba: A term used to refer to the women overseen by a tribal chief.

Ngoma: African term for a traditional dance.

Ngwazi: A Chewa word meaning "Savior," "Deliverer."

Nyasaland: The British colonial name used prior to Malawi.

Thangata: A colonial practice on estates similar to apartheid.

Thonje: A Chewa word meaning cotton.

Vellozia: A bush which grows in the Mulanje Massif.

Climbing Terms

Ascender: Clamped onto a rope allows sliding up the rope.

Belay: Climbing technique to protect a leader from a long fall.

Belay device: Object which increases holding power of belay.

Carabiner: An oval-shaped snap link used in climbing.

Climbing hardware: Special climbing gear e.g. nuts, carabiners.

Climbing harness: Safety harness connecting a climber to a rope.

Climbing Rope: Typically, 150=feet long, 11mm diameter, tests to 5000 pounds, used in securing a team while climbing.

Rock climbing shoes: Smooth soled shoes specifically for rock climbing.

Bibliography

BBC News Online. *Mandela expresses regret at Banda's death.* The British Broadcasting Corporation. London. November 27, 1997.

Benson, C.W. and F. M. Benson. *The Birds of Malawi.* Printed by Montford Press, Limbe, Malawi. 1974.

Eastwood, Frank. *Guide To The Mulanje Massif.* Lorton Publications. Johannesburg, Republic of South Africa. 1979. ISBN:0-620-03437-8

Maclean, Gordon Lindsay. *Robert's Birds of Southern Africa.* The Trustees of the John Voelcker Bird Book Fund. Cape Town, Republic of South Africa. Fifth Edition,1985. ISBN: 0-620-07681.

McMaster, Carolyn. *Malawi - Foreign Policy and Development.* Julian Friedmann Publishers Ltd. London, England. 1974. ISBN: 0-904014-03-7.

Ntara, Samuel Josia. *The History of the Chewa (Mbiri Ya Achewa).* Franz Steiner Verlag GMBH, Wiesbaden, Germany, 1973.

Short, Philip. *Banda.* Routledge & Kegan Paul, London and Boston. 1974. ISBN:0-7100-7631-2

Welensky, Sir Roy. *Welensky's 4000 Days : The Life and Death of the Federation of Rhodesia and Nyasaland.* Roy Publishers, Inc., New York. 1964.

Williams, David T. *Malawi The Politics of Despair.* Cornell University Press. Ithica and London. 1978. ISBN: 0-8014-1149-1

Author's Notes

Maps
Page 4: Africa 1890, from the Perry-Casteneda Library Map
Collection, On-line. The University of Texas at Austin. This
digital image is not copyright and may be reproduced. Credit also
to the original map maker, Rand, McNally & Co.

Page 82: Malawi 1964, by the author using Epi Map, Mapping
software from the Centers For Disease Control and Prevention.
Atlanta, Georgia, 1996.This digital image is not copyright and may
be reproduced.

Page 100: Climber's Malawi 1988, original by George Chilinda.
First reproduced in *Shadows on the Wall*. Reproduced with
modifications by permission of the author.

Chapter 4
Thanks to Philip Short for reporting about Banda's life through the
early 1970s, see reference. Ibid. for all other chapters on Banda's
life through that time period.

Chapter 10
These bird books are essential for Malawi birding, see references.

Chapter 23
Second paragraph - Information about Nelson Mandela from the
BBC, see reference.

Third paragraph - Thanks to Philip Short for reporting these
words, see reference.

Book Cover

Several sources contributed to the making of the final book cover. Thanks to Whitex Fabrics, Malawi, for making the beautiful cloth material commemorating the thirtieth anniversary of Kamuzu's return. A photograph of the cloth bust of Dr. Banda on this fabric is used on the front cover. Thanks to Joeff Davis who shot the photograph. The author photo was taken by Kim Jew Photography Studio who granted permission to reproduce this image on the back cover. The photograph of Chambe Peak is from the author's collection. Final book cover layout by the author.

Printed in the United States
20177LVS00001B/97-120